JUDITH McWILLIAMS

A PERFECT SEASON

Silhouette Desire

Originally Published by Silhouette Books
a division of
Harlequin Enterprises Ltd.

First published in Great Britain in 1990 by Silhouette Books, Eton House, 18-24 Paradise Road, Richmond, Surrey TW9 1SR

© Judith McWilliams 1990

Silhouette, Silhouette Desire and Colophon are Trade Marks of Harlequin Enterprises B.V.

ISBN 0 373 57898 9

22 – 9006

Made and printed in Great Britain

"Do You Want To Skip The Preliminaries And Go Directly To The Main Event?"

Jace's warm breath wafted over her cheeks. His handsome face broke into a sensual smile that sent Christina's heartbeat into overdrive.

"The main event is likely to be a fight if you don't let me go, Jason McCormick!" she retorted, trying to pull away.

"Christina Hollowell, do you mean to tell me that you're nothing more than a tease? Jumping into bed with a man and then refusing to deliver?"

"I did not jump into bed with you! I was ambushed by your shoes!"

"It was fate," he said with soulful emphasis. "You are obviously destined for my bed."

"In the first place, this is my bed, since it's in my house. And in the seond, what you're destined for is to hang!"

He gave her a hopeful look. "Does the condemned man get a last kiss?"

Dear Reader:

Welcome! You hold in your hand a Silhouette Desire – your ticket to a whole new world of reading pleasure.

As you might know, we are continuing the *Man of the Month* concept through to May 1991. In the upcoming year look for special men created by some of our most popular authors: Elizabeth Lowell, Annette Broadrick, Diana Palmer, Nancy Martin and Ann Major. We're sure you will find these intrepid males absolutely irresistible!

But Desire is more than the *Man of the Month*. Each and every book is a wonderful love story in which the emotional and sensual go hand-in-hand. A Silhouette Desire can be humourous or serious, but it will always be satisfying.

For more details please write to:

Jane Nicholls
Silhouette Books
PO Box 236
Thornton Road
Croydon
Surrey
CR9 3RU

JUDITH McWILLIAMS

began to enjoy romances while in search of the proverbial happily ever after. But she always found herself
rewriting the endings, and eventually the beginnings,
of the books she read. Then her husband finally suggested that she write one of her own, and she's been
doing so ever since. A former teacher with four children, Judith has traveled the country extensively with
her husband and has been greatly influenced by those
experiences. But when not tending the garden or
caring for family, Judith does what she enjoys most –
writing. She has also written under the name
Charlotte Hines.

Another Silhouette Book by Judith McWilliams

Silhouette Desire

Reluctant Partners

One

"But it'd do you good to go play tennis with me!" Bunny said in exasperation.

"Uh-huh," Christina muttered absently as she turned another page of the thick document on the desk in front of her.

"Will you put that damn thing down and listen to me?" Bunny demanded. "It's been two weeks since the funeral and you're still holed up in this house."

"But it's such a nice hole." Christina Hollowell's dark blue eyes warmed as she glanced around the study, her gaze lingering on the curio cabinet holding the extensive collection of jade her great-grandfather had acquired during the course of his diplomatic career in the Far East. "Besides, you have no idea of how much paperwork there is with the transfer of an estate the size that Elizabeth and Howard left," she added on a more practical note.

Bunny waved a dismissing hand. "That's what lawyers are for. Why not let them do their jobs?"

"Because when all's said and done, their estate is my responsibility. At least until Albert's twenty-five, and I prefer to know exactly what's going on with the things I'm responsible for."

Bunny shook her head. "You know, Christina, you're a total contradiction. I mean, look at you. A beautiful blue-eyed blonde wearing designer clothes, sitting in her family's mansion in the best section of Boston. By all rights you should be purely decorative and, instead, you're up to your elegant eyebrows in legal mumbo jumbo. And what's worse, you understand it!"

"Ah, an intelligent woman. Her price is above pearls." Christina's eyes glimmered with laughter at her friend's aggrieved expression.

"That's a virtuous woman and it's all your Aunt Margaret's fault."

"Aunt Margaret? I can see how my being virtuous could be blamed on my parents since they raised me, but Aunt Margaret?"

"Not being virtuous, being strange. And I guess in a way it was your parents' fault since they let you spend so much time with your aunt when you were young and impressionable."

"My Aunt Margaret is not strange! A little different perhaps..."

"They don't come more different than your Aunt Margaret. I mean, think about it. She has every bit as much money as your parents and instead of being content to make a splash in Boston society, she became a full professor at Harvard, decades before it was fashionable to have a token woman on the staff. And did she pick a nice feminine subject to teach? Not her. She's an authority on some eighteenth century nut.''

''Nineteenth, and Thoreau was not a nut. He was as ahead of his time as Aunt Margaret was. He was concerned about protecting the environment and being self-sufficient long before anyone else was.''

''And I keep telling you that being self-sufficient is not an excuse to spend all your time grubbing around in the dirt. If you want to be self-sufficient, go to the grocery store.''

''There's a fallacy in your argument big enough to drive a Mack truck through,'' Christina pointed out, too used to her friends' disdainful attitude toward her passion for growing things to feel hurt.

''I am not arguing with you. I wouldn't dare. You're...'' Bunny frowned as something outside one of the windows caught her eye. She squinted, trying to bring it into focus.

''Ha!'' Bunny snorted. ''Legal papers, indeed. No wonder you're so eager to get rid of me. You don't want to share the goodies. And what a goodie!'' She stared out the window and sighed rapturously. ''I'm getting goose bumps just looking at all those gorgeous muscles. My mind positively boggles at the idea of running my hands over them.''

''What are you blathering about?'' Christina tried to see around her, but Bunny had effectively blocked the view.

''I'm talking about the man climbing your front steps. He's totally awesome. Thick, dark brown hair, broad shoulders, flat stomach, muscular thighs. I wonder how big his—''

''Bunny!''

''Don't be a prude, Christina. You've probably thought the same thing yourself when you've looked at a fabulous physique. The only difference is that I'm honest enough to admit it.''

"There's a vast difference between outrageousness and honesty at your age—"

"I'm only twenty-nine."

"Thirty-two," Christina corrected her with a wicked smile. "You're exactly the same age as I am."

"There's nothing worse than an old friend with a long memory," Bunny mourned. "Well, if you won't play tennis with me, I guess I'll be going."

Christina grinned at her, having no illusions about Bunny's sudden decision to leave. "You'd better hurry if you're planning on picking up my visitor with the awesome body, because I told the housekeeper I wasn't seeing anyone today. She's liable to send your salesman on his way before you can make contact."

"Salesmen don't look like that. Besides, he can't go very fast. He's got some kind of a brace on his knee and he's limping."

"What!" The paper Christina had been holding fluttered unnoticed to the floor as the color faded from her flawless complexion.

"I said he's got something wrong with his leg," Bunny repeated, frowning in confusion as Christina rounded the huge mahogany desk and sprinted for the window.

"Damn!" Christina had no trouble recognizing the man who was awkwardly climbing the shallow brick steps to her front door.

She closed her eyes in a useless effort to deny her visitor's existence. She simply didn't feel up to coping with Jace McCormick right now.

"Exactly who is that delectable tidbit of masculinity?" Bunny demanded.

"You try munching on him and you'll wind up with ptomaine poisoning!"

"What's the matter? Doesn't he like blue-eyed blondes of independent means?" Bunny teased and then abruptly sobered when there was no answering smile. "All jokes aside, who is that guy, Christina?"

"Sort of a relation." Christina nervously chewed her lower lip. "My cousin, Howard, married that man's cousin, Elizabeth, which I think makes us both second cousins to their son, Albert."

"But I don't remember seeing tall, dark and handsome at their funeral."

"He was in the hospital with a knee injury," Christina said absently, much more concerned about why he was here now. Was it a duty call? To pay his condolences to Albert? But why bother to come all the way from California when a phone call would have sufficed?

"Listen, Christina, if you're worried, I'd be glad to see him for you."

Christina smiled indulgently at the openly calculating expression on Bunny's gamin features.

"I appreciate the sacrifice you're willing to make on my behalf, but I can't ask it of you. You can make your escape out the back while I go see him."

"All right, but if you change your mind, just yell. I'll walk slowly." Bunny accepted defeat gracefully.

Any cries Bunny heard would probably be caused by frustration, Christina thought glumly as she watched her friend leave. Jace McCormick was without doubt the most aggravating man she'd ever met.

"Miss Christina—" the housekeeper's voice intruded on her uneasy thoughts "—Mr. McCormick is here to see you. I made him comfortable in the small sitting room." Marta shook her graying head. "Poor boy, he looks quite tired."

"Then I'd better not keep him waiting." Christina got to her feet. The sooner she found out why Jace was here the sooner she could get rid of him.

Marta was right, Christina thought as she paused just outside the doorway of the sitting room and studied Jace with a critical eye. He did look tired. In fact, he looked ill. She frowned at the grayish tinge of his skin around his tightly compressed lips. Compressed because of pain or grief at the senseless waste of his cousin's life? She didn't know and it wasn't any of her business anyway, she reminded herself. Elizabeth's son was Christina's responsibility, not Elizabeth's cousin.

Determined to get the confrontation over with as soon as possible, she moved into the room.

"Good afternoon, Jace. It was good of you to call."

"Stow the 'grande dame' act, Christina. I didn't fly three thousand miles to be treated to your society manners," he said bluntly.

"You ought to be treated to someone's manners since you don't appear to have any of your own," Christina shot back. "Tell me, since we've decided to skip the pleasantries, why did you come?"

"For Albert, of course."

"Unfortunately, Albert isn't here right now. He's being tested this afternoon."

"Tested?" Jace frowned. "He wasn't involved in the accident. What's wrong with him?"

"Nothing, if you discount having lost his parents three weeks ago," she said dryly. "His school starts in a couple of weeks, and they do extensive tests beforehand so that they can plan each child's curriculum for the coming year."

"Good Lord, he's only in the fourth grade. What do they need to plan?"

"Modern education is—"

"Is in the process of producing a country of semi-illiterates."

"Over ninety-nine percent of the Walsingham Country Day School's graduates are accepted into the country's top prep schools." Christina repeated one of the statistics Howard had been so fond of quoting.

"But does Albert want to spend his boyhood being groomed for some elitist prep school?"

"His parents picked Walsingham and they were very happy with the job it was doing," Christina stated with perfect truth.

"His parents are dead. It's Albert's feelings which concern me now."

"Of course I welcome your concern for him—unexpected though it may be, when one considers the fact that you've had so little to do with him in the past," she added coolly.

"Not all of us inherited monstrous trust funds," he riposted. "Some of us have to earn a living."

"Considering the reputed size of your present contract, you're earning a living for half of Boston," she said tartly.

Jace opened his mouth, paused and then asked, "Why are we arguing?"

Christina shrugged. "Probably because we have a natural antipathy toward each other."

"Is that what you call it?" His eyes narrowed thoughtfully as his gaze slipped from her face down her neck to the curve of her small breasts, clearly outlined against the thin silk T-shirt she was wearing. To her dismay she could feel her nipples hardening under his heated glance—a reaction Jace noticed with a small smile of purely masculine satisfaction.

Refusing to give in to the impulse to cross her arms over her chest, she tried to take control of the fast-deteriorating conversation.

"Since Albert isn't here, and since you and I seem to be incapable of carrying on a rational discussion..."

"Would you care to try for a physical one?" Jace gave her a hopeful look that sent tiny pinpricks of excitement dancing over her skin while her heartbeat began a rapid tattoo.

"No, thank you." She emphatically denied her response. "I've never had any desire to be part of a crowd. Besides, you don't look like you could stand up to much physical contact."

He grinned at her. "I don't generally stand up for physical contact."

Christina swallowed uneasily at the surge of warmth his words sent racing through her.

"I'm sure you have a very practiced technique," she said repressively.

"Practice makes perfect." He chuckled and then in a lightning-swift change of mood asked, "How long will it take to get Albert ready? I'm on the twenty-one-day disabled list, and I want to use the time to get everything organized."

"I hardly think it's going to take you twenty-one days to tell Albert how sorry you are about the accident."

"No, to get him settled in my home." Jace shifted uncomfortably, wincing as he jarred his knee.

Christina stared at him in horror. "Surely you aren't suggesting that you take responsibility for Albert? You? The playboy of the baseball world? The very idea's laughable."

"Elizabeth trusted me to look after him."

"Howard trusted me."

"Elizabeth put it in her will."

"So did Howard."

"A boy needs a man's influence," Jace countered.

To do what, Christina wondered with a chill feeling of foreboding. To force him into what Jace would undoubtedly feel were traditional masculine pastimes, such as organized sports? Poor uncoordinated, undersized Albert wouldn't stand a chance. He'd spend his childhood covered with bruises and convinced he couldn't measure up. A surge of protective love shook her. That wasn't going to happen to Albert. Not while she had a breath left in her body.

"And how do you define a man?" she shot back. "Someone who spends his time flinging a little white ball around?"

"I realize my choice of profession may not meet your elevated standards, Miss Hollowell." He glared at her. "But then most of us weren't born with your advantages."

"Albert was," she said tightly, making no attempt to defend herself from his implied charge of snobbery.

"Then I'll just have to hope he can rise above them."

"If he went with you, it wouldn't be a question of rising anywhere, it would be how far he'd sink!"

"You are the most aggravating, pigheaded..." Jace jumped to his feet and in doing so caught his knee on the sharp edge of the coffee table. He froze, his face turning chalk white.

"Jace!" Confronted with his obvious pain, Christina's anger dissolved. "What's wrong? I thought orthoscopic surgery was supposed to be relatively painless?"

"It is." He released his pent up breath on a long, shuddering sigh and slowly unlocked his rigid limbs. "Unfortunately, the incision became infected and that's proving more of a problem than the surgery."

Christina stared at him. "Exactly when did you get out of the hospital?"

"This morning," he muttered.

She stared at him in disbelief. How could he have been so foolish as to leave the hospital and immediately fly three thousand miles to collect Albert. And all because of a promise he'd once made Elizabeth. Apparently he was capable of both love and loyalty. Not that she had any intention of letting him try to make Albert over in his image, but she did feel more charitable toward him.

"What are you plotting, Christina Hollowell?" Jace eyed her narrowly. "My demise?"

"Certainly not. You seem to be taking care of that all by yourself. You should be in bed. You look like hell," she said bluntly.

He grimaced. "Thanks for the testimonial. Now if you'll just agree—"

"No."

"Christina, be reasonable. When are you going to find time for Albert? You must run half the volunteer organizations in Boston."

"Make up your mind. A few minutes ago I was a parasitic lady of leisure. Not that your opinion makes any difference, but for your information I've taken a leave of absence from all my volunteer work so that I'll be here when Albert needs me."

"You mean so that you can smother him," Jace sniped.

About to respond in kind, Christina noticed the deepening lines besides his tightly compressed lips. Exchanging insults was not only futile, it was taking its toll on Jace's obviously depleted reserves of strength. He needed to rest. And she needed to see her lawyer to find out exactly what her legal position was if Jace persisted.

"I refuse to fight with you anymore today," she finally said.

"Well, that's a first," Jace muttered.

"Where's your luggage?" She ignored his provocative comment.

"In the taxi that's waiting for me out front. Why?"

"I'll have the driver bring it in when I pay him. You should go right up and lie down."

"Why are you inviting me to stay here?" He frowned consideringly at her.

"Why not?" She shrugged, refusing to delve beneath the surface of her impulse to keep him near. "You're part of Albert's family and this way you can see more of him. Besides, hotels can be pretty grim when you're sick."

"I'm not sick. I just have a little infection."

"Does this little infection come with medication?"

"Yes, nanny." He gave her a weary smile that unexpectedly tugged at her heartstrings.

"Good, then come on. I'll show you to a bedroom and you can take a nap before dinner." While I nip down and see my lawyer, she thought, trying to ignore the irrational feeling that she was going behind his back. All that mattered was that Albert be given the chance to grow into the best person he could be without being forced to conform to Jace's idea of what was acceptable male behavior, she told herself.

"Thank you for finding the time to see me on such short notice, Mr. Pauling." Christina sank down into the oversized leather chair in front of his desk. "I really appreciate it."

"How could you even think I might not?" He smiled, looking like a benevolent genie. "Our firm has represented your family for over two hundred years." He pressed his pudgy fingertips together and rested his chin on them. "Now then, you mentioned on the phone that this concerned young Albert?"

"Yes. Jace McCormick showed up this afternoon, and he seemed to feel that he has some right to be Albert's guardian."

"Unfortunately, he does." Mr. Pauling reached for the thick folder on his desk.

"Damn!" Christina bit off the exclamation in dismay. She'd been hoping that Mr. Pauling would laugh at Jace's claims and tell her that she had nothing to worry about.

"The problem is that Howard and Elizabeth each named a different guardian for Albert, and which will is valid depends on which one of them lived the longest."

Christina frowned. "I don't understand."

"You see, if Elizabeth died first, then everything she possessed, including the joint guardianship of Albert, passed to her husband. Then when Howard died, his will naming you Albert's guardian would be the valid one. Unfortunately, the reverse is also true."

"But how can we determine that? They died in a car accident in northern Japan."

"That's the problem." Mr. Pauling sighed. "We can't really say who predeceased whom. I've already checked into it. A passing farmer was the first at the scene of the accident, and both Howard and Elizabeth were dead when he found them. There's no way of determining who died first."

"So what do we do? I have no intention of handing Albert over to some overage adolescent who divides his time between baseball and chasing anything in a skirt."

"Are you that attached to Albert, or are you that opposed to Mr. McCormick?" Mr. Pauling asked shrewdly.

"A combination of both, I suppose." Christina rubbed her forehead, which was beginning to ache. "I dearly love Albert, but it's more like the love of an indulgent aunt, not that of a mother. He already had a loving mother; he didn't need a surrogate one. If I actually thought that it was in his best interests to live with Jace then I'd drop all claims to his guardianship in exchange for liberal visitation rights. But Jace McCormick is not a fit person to be responsible for a small boy. He..."

She paused as something suddenly occurred to her. Could Jace's interest in Albert be in the money he'd just inherited rather than in the boy himself?

"I know Jace is supposed to be making fantastic sums as a pitcher, but it's just as easy to spend fantastic sums, too. Could he be hoping to bleed Albert's trust fund?"

Mr. Pauling shook his head. "It's highly probable. When the accident occurred, I was afraid something like this might happen and I looked into Mr. McCormick's affairs."

"And?" Christina demanded.

"I found nothing that could be used against him in a custody dispute. He's invested his funds quite well. In fact, his monetary worth rivals yours," Mr. Pauling said approvingly. "On a personal level, he has an active social life, but since he's a bachelor, the courts won't hold that against him; he's well-known in the Los Angeles area for his support of a variety of charities, and he's the hero of half the young boys in America. In short, if Jason McCormick has any unsavory habits, he's keeping them well under wraps."

"Are you trying to tell me that I'd lose in a custody fight?" she asked anxiously.

"No. I'm telling you we don't want it to come to a court battle," he said patiently. "The best thing to do would be to negotiate with him. It's been my experience that people make all kinds of impossible vows when somebody they love dies. Once the emotionalism fades, they realized the impossibility of living up to them. Mr. McCormick's wanting Albert could well fall into that category. From what I could find out, he has absolutely no experience in the day-to-day

care of children. Upon closer acquaintanceship with Albert
he might find that being a parent is not all a bed of roses."

"I see," Christina said slowly. "What you say makes
sense."

"And it will also show you in the light of being a reasonable person if, God forbid, this should go to court."

"Thank you, Mr. Pauling." Christina rose. "You've
certainly given me a lot to think about."

"Hopefully, you'll be able to work something out with
Mr. McCormick, because if he were willing, he could open
a lot of doors for Albert in the future."

"And they'd all lead to the locker room!" she said
scathingly.

"Perhaps." He walked Christina across the office and
opened the door for her. "But remember that the old school
tie can extend into unexpected places. Now be sure to call me
if you run into any problems."

"I will." Christina gave him a preoccupied smile as she
left, her mind on the task in front of her. Somehow, she had
to convince Jace that his sudden burst of cousinly love was
liable to do Albert more harm than good. And she had to do
it without further upsetting Albert's precarious sense of security. She was already concerned about how Albert was
adjusting to the crushing blow that fate had dealt him. She
didn't even want to consider what might happen if he felt
that what little security he had left was being threatened.

Damn Jace McCormick, she thought angrily as she
climbed into her car. Why couldn't he have stayed in California where he belonged.

The first person she saw when she arrived home was Albert. He had obviously been watching for her, because he
erupted through the front door the second she stopped the
car.

"Christina, did you see him? Did you see him?" Albert was literally hopping from foot to foot in his excitement. "Marta says that my cousin, Jace, is here. Right in this very house! Now they'll have to believe me."

Christina refused to acknowledge the unexpected surge of jealousy that engulfed her at his ecstatic words. Small boys had been idolizing sports figures since time immemorial, she told herself. It didn't lessen Albert's affection for her.

She gave him a quick hug. "Who'll have to believe you?"

"The boys at school. When I tried out for the baseball team last spring, the coach said I had two left feet." Albert followed Christina into the house. "And everyone laughed, and I told them Jace McCormick was my cousin, and they said I was lying."

"I didn't know you wanted to play baseball." Christina pushed back a lock of the ash-blond hair hanging in his eyes.

"I didn't tell anyone so if I didn't make the team, Dad wouldn't know I blew it."

"But, Albert, is isn't whether you win or lose that's important. It's that you tried your best."

"Yeah, the teacher's always say that to the losers, but they never say it to the winners."

Christina had to admit he did have a point, although this wasn't the best time to debate it. There were far too many other problems to be addressed. And first in line was figuring out a method for getting rid of Jace McCormick. She glanced around the spacious entry hall, wondering if he was still upstairs lying down.

"Albert, have you actually seen Jace?"

"No, Marta said he was tired and was resting. But I don't see why he needs to rest in the middle of the afternoon."

Christina glanced down at his puzzled face. Jace McCormick might infuriate her, but he had left the hospital and come directly to see Albert, and Albert had a right to know that. He had so few relatives left in the world, he deserved to know that those few loved him and valued him.

"Albert, Jace is tired because he's been in hospital in California. He only got out this morning."

"And he came right to visit me?" Albert's thin little chest puffed out with pride.

"Uh-huh. Your mother was his favorite cousin." Never mind that she was his only cousin, Christina thought cynically. "So, of course, her little boy would be extra special to him. Now, then, how did today's testing go?"

"Not so great." He shrugged his narrow shoulders despondently. "Mr. Baxter yelled at me because I hadn't done my summer reading. I was going to do it right before the test so I'd remember it all, but then . . ." He gulped and his eyes filled with tears.

"Never mind." Christina put her arms around him. "I'm sure your teacher didn't realize—"

"Oh, yes, he did," Albert muttered into her shoulder. "Mr. Baxter said it was a shame about . . . about what happened, but if I'd planned properly, I'd have already done the reading."

"I'll plan him!" Christina said in outrage at such a callous attitude. "What kind of unfeeling monster is this Mr. Baxter?"

"He's the football coach for the senior division," Albert said dejectedly. "He said that a real man has to face up to what life throws at him."

"You aren't a man." Christina dropped a kiss on his head. "You're a boy. The rules are different for boys."

"Not at Walsingham." Albert gave her a pitying look. "Walsingham builds men."

"That's the Marine Corps," Christina said dryly. "What was it you were supposed to have read?"

"Moby Dick," he said glumly.

"Moby Dick?" She frowned. "That hardly seems like an appropriate book for a nine-year-old."

"It's because I'm gifted. I have to be challenged," he rattled off what were obviously oft-repeated words.

Christina opened her mouth and then closed it when she found she had nothing to say. There was a lot going on here that she didn't understand, and the sooner she got over to that school and had a heart-to-heart talk with the headmaster, the better. But not today. She drew a tired breath. Today she had to figure out how to placate Jace without actually giving him what he wanted.

She jumped as the antique grandfather clock in the hallway began to chime the hour. "Goodness, I didn't realize it was so late, Albert. Why don't you wash your hands while I see if Jace feels up to joining us for dinner."

"I'll hurry." Albert clattered up the wide stairway, and Christina followed him more slowly, drawn as if by a magnet to Jace's room.

She paused outside his door and ran her suddenly damp palms down over her linen slacks. Come on, Christina, you aren't some impressionable teenager. You're a thirty-two-year-old woman—who might as well be a teenager considering the effect Jace had on her, she thought in resignation. It made no sense, but from the moment she'd first met him four years ago at a party Howard and Elizabeth had given, she'd felt a wave of attraction. It was as if her body recognized and responded to him on a level that transcended rational thought. It was a feeling she'd instantly rejected. She'd seen the all too common result of such mindless sexual reaction while working at the battered women's shelter. She knew better than to ever trust such a potent response when it wasn't reinforced by a basic sense of liking and respect for the man himself.

Fortunately, because of Jace's busy schedule, Howard and Elizabeth had almost always visited him in California. He hadn't been in Boston more than half a dozen times since she'd first met him.

And at the moment, she sincerely wished he'd come one time less. She grimaced at the closed door. Taking a deep breath, she gently rapped on the gleaming cherry panel.

"Go away." Jace's sleepy voice was barely audible through the thick wood.

Christina ignored the command. Jace needed to eat as much as he needed to sleep, and, besides, Albert would explode if Jace didn't appear at dinner.

She pushed open the door and stepped inside. The heavy rose silk drapes had been pulled across the long narrow windows, encasing the room in an intimate dusky light.

The sound of her footsteps was swallowed up in the thick Aubusson carpet. She paused at the foot of the centuries-old four-poster bed, her mouth drying as she stared down at him. His dark brown hair was tousled and his eyes were closed. Compulsively her eyes traced over the lean planes of his cheeks, down along his square jaw to land on his firm lips, which were slightly parted.

"Jace..." To her intense annoyance, her voice cracked and she coughed to disguise the fact. "Jace, it's time to get up," she tried again.

When she didn't get an answer, she started around the side of the bed, intending to give him a gentle shake. Unfortunately, in the dim light she failed to see his shoes and tripped over them. A startled cry escaped her as she pitched forward, landing sprawled beside him.

His arms closed around her as she tried to scramble off the bed.

Christina shut her eyes in negation of the entire situation. An action that seemed only to make her more aware of the tangy scent of his cologne, of the warmth his body was generating and of the unyielding feel of his muscles pressing against hers.

She swallowed uneasily and forced her eyes open to find herself staring into the sleepy depths of his.

"Why, Christina," his husky voice rasped through her agitated mind, "I didn't realize you cared."

"I came to wake you up," she muttered, disconcerted by the melting sensation she could feel spreading through her. She tried to sit up, but his arms merely tightened, and rather than allow the situation to degenerate into an undignified scuffle that would undoubtedly hurt his knee and her pride, she stayed where she was.

"I thought it was the prince who was supposed to wake up Sleeping Beauty with a kiss. Not the other way around." His warm breath touched her cheeks, causing the skin to tighten.

"You're not a prince," she retorted, trying to distance her mind if not her body."

"But you're certainly a beauty." He laughed and her body absorbed the feel of his amusement.

"Stop flirting with me." Christina demanded, denying her instinctive response.

"You want to skip the preliminaries and go directly to the main event?" He gave her a sensual smile that sent her heartbeat into overdrive, even though her mind knew he was only teasing.

"The main event is likely to be a fight if you don't let me go, Jason McCormick!"

"Christina Hollowell, do you mean to tell me that you're nothing more than a tease? Jumping into bed with a man and then refusing to deliver."

"I did not jump into bed with you!" she said through gritted teeth. "I was ambushed by your shoes."

"It was fate," Jace said with a soulful emphasis that undermined her resolve to hold herself aloof. "You are obviously destined for my bed."

"In the first place, this is my bed, since it's in my house, and in the second, what you're destined for is to hang."

"Does the condemned man get a last kiss?" He gave her a hopeful look.

"Oh, for pity's sake." Christina dropped a quick kiss on the corner of his mouth, almost losing her already shaky composure as his warmth touched her lips.

"Now get up," she ordered, tearing herself out of his arms and scrambling off the bed, no longer caring if she appeared gauche or not. All that mattered was that she escape the feel of his body.

"Dinner is in fifteen minutes," she threw at him from the door. "Please don't be late. Albert would be disappointed."

"But you wouldn't, would you?" Jace eyed her shrewdly. "It would suit you just fine if I disappeared and never showed my face again."

"Nonsense." She forced a calm tone. "As one of Albert's few relatives you'll always be welcome to visit us."

"I'll be sure to return the favor when Albert is living with me."

Christina pressed her lip against a telling retort and escaped with what dignity she could salvage.

Two

Can I have some more chocolate cake, Christina?" Albert eyed the thick fudge icing with unadulterated greed.

"Certainly." She cut him a second slice, elated at even this small sign of the return of his normally voracious appetite. She glanced over at Jace's virtually untouched plate. He'd eaten almost nothing, merely going through the motions of rearranging the food on his plate.

"When I'm done, I'm going to call all the guys and tell them Jace is here," Albert said around a mouthful of cake.

"Don't talk with your mouth full," Christina automatically corrected him, her attention still focused on Jace. He was definitely paler than he'd been half an hour ago, and there were deeply carved lines beside his mouth. He looked as if he should go back to bed.

Alone, she chided herself, appalled at the surge of sensation that flooded her at the memory of his body pressed up against hers. What was it about this man that enabled him to press all her hidden buttons without even being aware that he was doing so, she wondered uneasily. Her reaction certainly wasn't mutual. She remembered the teasing glints in his eyes when he'd held her earlier. There'd been no overwhelming sense of awareness in them. Which was good, she assured herself. The present situation was complicated enough. It didn't need mutual sexual attraction added to it.

"Can the guys come over and see Jace tonight? Please Christina," Albert begged.

"Let's wait until tomorrow," Christina suggested. "Jace really should spend the evening resting."

"At least I got supper before I was sent to my room," Jace grumbled.

"Not that you bothered to eat any of it." She glanced significantly at his crumbled cake.

"But Jace can't go to bed. It's light out." Albert sounded scandalized. "And not only that, but his team is playing the Cubs and it's on WGN."

"There's no reason for him to miss it," Christina soothed Albert. "There's a TV in his room. He can watch the game until he falls asleep." Which might not be all that long, Christina thought with a sideways glance at Jace. He looked as if the only thing holding him upright was sheer willpower.

"I guess so," Albert said sadly, and Christina's eyes narrowed as an idea suddenly occurred to her. Jace was about to learn that taking care of kids was not all fun and games. That their needs had to be met even when you yourself felt miserable.

"Why don't you watch the game with Jace, Albert? The bed's certainly big enough for you to sit beside him, and that way he can explain all the good parts to you." She gave Jace an innocent smile.

"I'd love to explain all the good parts to you, too." Jace returned the smile with interest. "Better yet, I'll demonstrate them."

"Will you show me how to throw a fork ball, Jace?" Albert begged, oblivious to the adult undercurrents.

"I think Jace speaks with forked tongue," Christina muttered.

"Tomorrow I'll show you how to hold the ball, Albert, but I can't do any actual pitching until my knee heals."

"How long will that be?" Albert demanded.

"Well, the surgeon's not willing to commit himself to an actual date, and this infection set it back, but I'm on the twenty-one-day disabled list, which is why—"

"Albert," Christina hurriedly interrupted, afraid that Jace was about to blurt out his intention of dragging Albert off to California, "why don't you go tune in the ball game. It should have already started."

"Sure," Albert happily agreed.

Christina waited until Albert was out of the room before turning to Jace. "Don't you dare upset him."

"He isn't the least bit upset. He's bubbling over with anticipation at the thought of exhibiting me to his friends. Rather like a hunting trophy," Jace said ruefully.

"It has nothing to do with you personally," Christina insisted.

"Of course not," Jace promptly agreed. "Albert doesn't know me as a person yet. But he will." His words had the ring of a vow. "I'm a firm believer in beginning as you mean to go on."

"It's a good thing for you I'm not," Christina snapped, "or you'd be wearing your dessert instead of playing with it."

"Christina, you aren't thinking—"

"I'm thinking of Albert, which is a darn sight more than you're doing."

"Why not let Albert do his own thinking," Jace shot back. "The boy's old enough to decide who he wants to live with. Or are you afraid he'd choose me."

"As you so succinctly pointed out, he doesn't know you. If he did choose you, he'd have simply been seduced by your profession," she said bitterly. "However, you do have a point."

"Only one?"

"Besides the one on top of your head!"

"Speaking of points . . ." His eyes dropped to her breasts clearly outlined against the thin material of her blouse.

To her dismay, she could feel the tips hardening under the impact of his devouring gaze. Ignoring what she didn't seem to be able to help, she doggedly continued, "Your invitation to California—"

"Indiana," Jace interrupted her.

"Indiana?" She blinked. "I thought you lived in California?"

"I do most of the time, but that's only out of necessity. I consider the farm in central Indiana my real home. I intend to live there when I retire."

"Farm?" Christina stared at him in surprise. Nothing she'd ever read or heard about him had given the least inkling that he had an interest in anything other than the amusements to be found in a large city.

"This conversation is never going to get anywhere if you can't bring yourself to contribute anything original."

"Sorry," she muttered. "I just can't see you as a farmer."

"But then, like Albert, you don't know the real me, do you? Would you agree to letting Albert visit me while I'm recuperating so that he can get to know me?"

"You won't mention that you want to make the visit permanent?"

"Not at the moment," he said slowly.

"In that case, since Albert is the one most directly involved, I think it only fair that he be given some say in the decision," she finally said.

"Without being made to feel guilty about it?"

"I do not play emotional blackmail games!"

"You don't play emotional games at all, do you?" Jace said shrewdly. "What happened, Christina? Were you badly burned once?"

"You're the one who's going to get burned if you don't drop it."

"But—"

"I hesitate to deflate your attempt at amateur psychology, but I have never been the victim of a blighted love affair," she said.

"Then why do you react like a scalded cat whenever I get too close?"

"I do not!" she insisted, stung at his unflattering description.

"You wouldn't happen to be afraid of me, would you?" He gave her a penetrating look.

"No, although I will admit to having some qualms about what I might do *to* you if you don't give up this wild scheme of yours."

"I'm not giving it up and it isn't the least bit wild. The psychiatrist I talked to said—"

"Psychiatrist?" Christina stared at him in surprise. She hadn't expected Jace to even consider Albert's emotional state of mind, let alone go to the trouble of consulting a psychiatrist. That he had thought about it seemed to give added seriousness to his demand for custody. She swallowed uneasily.

"Yes, psychiatrist," Jace said irritably. "I know you think all athletes have the sensitivity of a block of wood, but—"

"No, not all of them," Christina sniped and immediately felt ashamed of herself. "I'm sorry," she apologized. "That was a cheap shot and wasn't true besides. It's just that I'm already worried about Albert, and from my point of view you're simply one more complication."

"I don't suppose you could bring yourself to view me as part of the solution? I—"

"The game's about to start, Jace." Albert erupted into the room. "And guess what. The announcer was talking about you. He said you're recuperating in California."

"Not California—" Jace began.

"Albert," Christina broke in at the determined look on Jace's face. She'd agreed to let Albert decide about Jace's invitation himself and she would, but she wanted to be the one to present the idea. Who knew what Jace might blurt out.

"Yes?" Albert turned to her with barely concealed impatience, and she stifled a sigh. It was starting already. Albert couldn't see beyond the media image to the man beneath.

"Jace and I have something we'd like to discuss with you. Since he can't play baseball for a few weeks, he's going to recuperate on his farm and he'd like you to visit him."

"Me?" Albert's eyes widened, and a look of such incredulous delight washed over his face that Christina felt her heart sink. There seemed little doubt what his decision would be.

"You want me to visit you?" He turned to Jace as if he couldn't believe the invitation had actually been issued.

"Well, actually, Albert—"

"Of course he does," Christina hurriedly interrupted, afraid that Jace was about to say something about making the visit permanent, promise or no promise.

"Oh, boy!" Albert hopped from one foot to the other. "Wait till I tell the guys. Just wait—" He suddenly frowned.

"You're coming too, aren't you, Christina?" Albert scooted closer to her.

Christina felt as if a great weight had been lifted off her shoulders. Albert was not so infatuated with Jace that he was willing to abandon their long-standing relationship.

"She's certainly been invited." Jace uttered the bald-faced lie without a blink. "But do you think she'd be willing to leave Boston? She's kind of settled here."

"And miss a chance to visit you?" Christina's look of wide-eyed innocence was a masterpiece. Jace wasn't going to get rid of her that easily. At least if she went along, she could make sure nothing happened to Albert. And considering what she'd read about Jace in the scandal sheets, it seemed more than likely that he'd promptly forget that he was responsible for Albert if he happened to meet a willing woman.

"Christina and I would love to visit you," Albert said slowly, confused by the undercurrents he could hear but couldn't understand.

"Then it's settled." To Christina's astonishment, Jace also caught the unease in Albert's voice and promptly moved to erase it. "We'll leave in the morning. The three of us." He shot Christina a speculative look that made her very nervous. He obviously hadn't liked her inviting herself along, but she didn't care. Albert was the only thing that mattered, and she fully intended on being present to make sure he didn't suffer any more emotional knocks.

* * *

"Do you suppose that's the Monongahela River?" Albert squashed his small nose up against the airplane's window.

"Perhaps. It's in the right general area," Jace replied with a continued patience that surprised Christina. For the past hour and a half he'd been calmly answering a steady stream of questions. At first she'd made no attempt to deflect them, hoping that Albert's constant chatter would begin to dim Jace's rosy glow of parenthood. But Jace's patience was making her reevaluate her impression of him.

She glanced over at him, frowning as she noticed his increasing pallor and the furtive way he was rubbing his thigh, almost as if his knee were too painful to touch. Christina stifled a sigh. Albert wasn't the only one who needed protecting. Jace needed protection from his own inability to admit that he wasn't well. She never should have let him make his trip the day after he'd arrived. Although how she could have stopped him . . . Christina sighed again.

She was fast discovering that Jace McCormick had a will of iron. When he decided he was going to do something, he did it, doggedly overcoming any obstacles in his path—a characteristic that didn't seem to mesh with the playboy image the press consistently presented of him. Nor had his patient response to Albert's questions seemed in character. She felt confused and at a distinct disadvantage, as if she were playing a game without knowing all the rules.

"Then could that be the Ohio?" Albert pointed toward the ground.

"Albert—" Christina moved to divert his attention from Jace "—why this sudden interest in rivers?"

"Oh, they're on my list."

"List? What list?"

"This one." Albert pulled several typed sheets from his backpack and handed them to her.

Christina glanced down at them. "Where'd you get this?"

"School. I called Mr. Baxter last night to tell him I couldn't come in next week to give my report on *Moby Dick*, like you told me to. He said my trip was an excellent chance to do some field research and that he'd drop off a list of questions for me in our mailbox this morning on his way over to the school. He did." Albert sighed.

"Field research? In the summer?" Jace sounded outraged. "Let me see that." He took the sheets out of her hand.

Christina tensed against the shimmer of excitement that skittered over her as his fingers brushed against hers.

"For pity's sake," Jace muttered as he read the list. "Albert, do you want to do this?"

"Of course not." The boy seemed surprised at the question.

"Then don't do it." Jace tore the sheets up and deposited the pieces in the litterbag on the back of the seat in front of him.

"Mr. Baxter isn't going to like that." Albert was clearly caught between joy at having gotten rid of the assignment and fear of the consequences.

"You leave Mr. Baxter to me," Christina said, for once in agreement with Jace's high-handed methods. "And you can consign *Moby Dick* to a watery grave, too."

"I could leave it in the bathroom. I got to go anyway," Albert suggested, clearly intent on getting rid of the book before she changed her mind. He pulled it out of his case and scrambled over Christina and Jace.

"Do you want the window seat, Jace?" she offered. "Albert can sit on the aisle for a while."

"No, Albert likes to look out and, besides, I have more room this way."

"Also more pain. That's at least the tenth time he's climbed over you."

"I'll survive."

"At what cost," Christina said, inexplicably annoyed at his refusal to take the easy way out. "Didn't that hospital give you anything for the pain in your knee?"

"They offered, but I don't like to take drugs," Jace said tiredly, tensing as Albert approached.

"Be careful of Jace's leg, Albert," Christina said sharply.

"Does it hurt?" Albert edged past him with exaggerated care.

"Yes, it hurts," Christina answered for Jace when it appeared that he was about to shrug the question off. "So let's try real hard to be still while he rests."

"Okay," Albert quickly agreed, and, pulling a comic book out of his backpack, settled down to read.

Christina stared blindly out the window at the fluffy white clouds, not really understanding her impulse to protect Jace when it would be in her own and ultimately Albert's best interests to have subtly urged the boy to make a pest of himself.

Thoughtfully she chewed her lower lip. She might be behaving out of character, but then so was Jace. He was turning out to be full of surprises. Such as his refusal to take drugs, even for something as relatively harmless as pain relief. She'd read so much about the free and easy use of drugs in professional sports that his attitude was totally unexpected.

Christina leaned her head back against the seat. The more she discovered about the man, the more complicated he seemed. Ah, well, she thought as she closed her eyes, she'd worry about it later. Once they were actually on Jace's farm, she'd be able to assess the situation and decide how to handle it. Maybe she ought to take a page out of Mr. Baxter's book and make a list. A reluctant smile curved her lips at the thought.

To her relief, by the time they were actually on the ground at the Indianapolis International Airport, Jace was beginning to look slightly better. The grayish tinge underlying his tan had faded somewhat, although it was clear that his knee was still bothering him. Rather unexpectedly, he made no objections when she all but ordered him to sit down in the lobby while she retrieved their luggage. Instead, he muttered a brusque thank-you and limped toward the seats, trailed by an excited Albert.

Fortunately the airplane was unloaded promptly, and she was able to rejoin Jace and Albert fifteen minutes later with their cases piled on a cart.

"Can I push the cart, Christina?" Albert bounded out of his chair.

"Sure, but go slowly. I'm wearing heels." Christina offered the excuse more from a desire to spare Jace's knee than from any awkwardness on her part.

"And very nice ones, too," Jace commented as his eyes wandered down the slim length of her calf visible beneath her soft silk skirt.

His scrutiny sent a surge of pleasure coiling through her. He obviously found her attractive—as he would *any* other reasonably pretty woman, she quickly reminded herself. But it was difficult to maintain the thought in the face of his obvious appreciation. Unwittingly Albert helped her to regain her sense of perspective by providing a diversion.

"Christina, look. See that neat rocket launcher. Isn't it incredible?"

"Sorry, I'm not into violence."

"That's not the impression I got," Jace whispered as Albert ran over to the shop's display window for a closer look.

"There's violence and there's violence." She looked down her nose at him.

"Now that's a concept worth exploring. Do you know that some psychologists claim that the act of making love is a form of sublimated violence?"

"Do you know that you talk too much?"

"Does that mean you'd prefer action?" Jace gave her an impossibly innocent look.

"It means I'd prefer a change of topic." Christina tried to ignore the sensation curling through her at the very idea of making love to him.

Albert rushed back to them. "The rocket launcher is only forty-two dollars. I want it."

"Sorry, my friend," Christina said. "That's an outrageous price for a few bits of cheap plastic."

"I don't think so," Albert argued. "I'll use my own money."

"Yours?" Christina frowned. "How much do you have on you?"

"Not that money. My trust fund money. That lawyer who talked to me said I had almost a million dollars a year income from the trust that Dad left me."

"It's called a trust fund because your father trusted me to keep it safe for you until you've grown up," Christina said.

"Aw, c'mon, Christina. Forty-two dollars isn't going to make any difference. And it is my money."

"No." Jace's crisp voice brooked no argument. "That money belongs to your father's estate until you turn twenty-five. If you want money to waste on junk, there's always jobs around the farm you can do to earn it."

"Earn it!"

Albert stared at Jace as if he'd never seen him before. As perhaps he hadn't, Christina thought shrewdly. Albert was just beginning to penetrate the public facade of the sports figure to realize that there was a very definite personality behind it. And, seemingly, a fair one. It would have been very easy for Jace to have overridden her decision and bought the toy, thus gaining popularity points in his quest for Albert's guardianship, but he hadn't.

Why hadn't he? she wondered. Because he thought she was right? Or because he thought that appearing to share her views on child raising would make her more inclined to agree to give him custody of Albert? The whole incident made her very uneasy. It was much simpler to outwit an opponent who was predictable. Jace was proving to be anything but.

"How are we getting from here to wherever it is we're going?" Christina decided to focus on a question she could get an answer to.

"My farm's outside Clinton, a little town not far from the Illinois border. It's about an hour and a half's drive. I called the man who looks after things for me when I'm not there and had him bring my car up yesterday and leave it here at the airport."

"I'll drive," Christina said with a quick glance at his leg.

To her relief, instead of arguing, he merely nodded. "The parking lot's through there." He started toward their left and Christina followed him, trailed by the still grumbling Albert.

"That's an Indiana farmhouse?" Christina stared in disbelief at the large house directly in front of her.

"Since it's located on a farm in Indiana, one could be forgiven for thinking so," Jace said dryly.

"You may have left California physically, but you definitely brought the architecture along with you."

"I kind of like it." Albert leaned over the front seat to get a better look.

"I do, too," Christina admitted. "It's just that you must admit it's a bit of a shock. I mean, first we travel six miles on a rutted gravel dirt road that couldn't have had more than four houses on it and then turn into a paved driveway to find this." She waved her hand at the sprawling structure. "At least the barn fits the image of a midwestern farm." She nodded toward the huge white structure several hundred feet behind the house.

"What do you have in your barn, Jace?" Albert asked eagerly. "Horses, cows, chickens?"

"Nothing. It's a lot less trouble to buy meat and eggs at the grocery store than it is to raise it. Besides," he admitted sheepishly, "I never could eat someone I was acquainted with."

"My sentiments exactly." Christina smiled at him.

"I'll be back in a minute. I want to look around." Albert tumbled out of the car and began to run toward the barn.

"Albert!" Christina yelled after him. "Don't you dare touch anything."

"There's nothing he can hurt."

"I'm not worried about the damage he might do. I'm worried about the damage that might be done to him."

"Boys are always breaking things." Jace started limping toward the house.

"As long as those things aren't part of Albert." Christina hurried after him.

Jace glanced at her tense features and asked, "What's really bothering you, Christina?"

"Do you want an itemized list or will a general overview do?" she snapped, all her doubts and uncertainties about the situation she found herself in momentarily showing.

"You aren't going to turn out to be a complainer, are you?"

"If the situation warrants it." She took a deep breath, trying to cool her flushed face. "If you hadn't been so pig-headed we'd still be back in Boston and I wouldn't be worried about Albert breaking his neck."

"Tell you what." Jace inserted a key in the heavy oak door. "I'm a fair man. You may have one complaint a day."

"One! The heat alone merits a dozen. It must be a hundred degrees out here." She pulled her shirt away from her back where it felt like it was glued to her body.

"Restraint is good for the soul." Jace grinned at her.

"I don't like—"

"Sorry, you've already had today's complaint. You'll have to save that one for tomorrow. In you go." He pushed open the door and motioned her inside.

Christina expelled her breath on a long happy sigh as the cool air reached out to engulf her with benevolent arms. "Thank God for central air conditioning."

"No, thank Watkins Plumbing and Heating." Jace dropped his keys on the black lacquered chest to the left of the door.

"You belong in bed," Christina inadvertently spoke her thoughts aloud.

"Is that an offer?" Jace's chocolate-brown eyes gleamed with sudden interest.

"No, it's the voice of common sense," she said tartly, as much in negation of his words as in the sudden surge of longing she felt. Much as she hated to admit it, her attraction to Jace was growing, and if she wasn't careful, it could cause horrendous complications in an already overly complicated situation.

Purposefully making her voice brisk, she said, "Why don't you take a nap while I drive back to that little town we passed through and try to find a grocery store."

"It isn't necessary. I had the man who looks after the place lay in a supply of groceries, and I can't sleep now. I need to make a few phone calls."

"Suit yourself." She gave a credible imitation of a nonchalant shrug. "If you manage to kill yourself, it'll simply save me a lot of hassle over Albert."

"Your concern is touching."

"You're no concern of mine."

"Is any man?" Jace eyed her narrowly. "Or is the reason you're still unattached because you're looking for a 'faire and perfect knight?'"

"Nope. I have a feeling a saint would be hell to live with and, furthermore, simply because I'm your houseguest—"

"Self-invited."

"Doesn't give you the right to delve into my love life." She ignored the interruption, as well as the small prick of hurt his comment caused.

"It does if it affects Albert," Jace insisted.

"Why, you hypocrite! I'm not the darling of the scandal sheets. Your sexual exploits are a terrible example to a young boy."

"Good God, Christina! Surely you aren't naive enough to believe what you read in those rags?" He looked dumbfounded.

"I'm not naive, period," she snapped. "A fact you'd do well to remember. Now if you won't go to bed, at least sit down before you fall down and I have to drag your senseless body through the house."

"Whatever happened to gentle, comforting women?" Jace grumbled.

"They went the way of the 'faire and perfect knight.'" Christina grinned at him, inordinately pleased to have gotten in the last word.

Three

———

Christina paused inside the dusky light of the huge barn and peered around, looking for Albert. She'd seen him go in, but now she couldn't find him. Maybe she was being overly protective, but as far as she knew, Albert had never been on a farm before. He'd have no idea of the dangers lying in wait for the unwary. After what had happened to his parents, she couldn't bear the thought of Albert being hurt.

"Albert, are you in here?"

"Up here."

Christina jumped as his voice seemed to materialize from above her head. Peering up, she saw Albert's small face framed in a large opening in the ceiling. "Come down from there before you fall and break your neck," she ordered.

"Aw, Christina, don't fuss." Albert clattered down a wide set of stairs built into the far wall that she hadn't noticed before. "I was just up in the hayloft, and guess what?" His blue eyes glowed with excitement.

"What?" she asked indulgently.

"I saw someone."

"In the hayloft?" She glanced upward, instinctively moving closer to Albert.

"No," he said impatiently. "Outside. Through the window. A boy my size. He was in the field behind the barn. I wonder what he was doing there?"

"He's probably just as curious about us as you are about him. Why don't you ask Jace if he knows who lives around here. I could visit his family and invite the boy over."

"Oh, no!" Albert viewed her with unfeigned horror. "He'd think that I was a baby and couldn't make friends by myself."

"I see," Christina said, seeing nothing of the sort, but recognizing panic when she heard it. "Tell you what. We could put a mantrap out in the field where you saw him and, when he gets caught, you could make his acquaintance when you let him go."

"Where could we get a mantrap?" Albert's face lit up with enthusiasm.

"I don't know, but now that I think about it, from what I remember of my history, mantraps were rather messy affairs. Maybe it'd be better if you simply walked up to him and introduced yourself."

"I've tried that before at home, but it doesn't work," he said gloomily. "They just stare at you as if they couldn't care less what your name is. I guess I'm not very interesting. But Jace is." Albert's eyes narrowed thoughtfully. "Everybody likes Jace."

"No, everybody does not like Jace. Everyone likes the media image of Jace. And that's not the same thing at all," she said, trying to make him understand.

"Maybe," Albert muttered, either not grasping or not caring about the distinction. "I think I will ask Jace about that boy. Where is he?"

"In the house making some phone calls."

"Oh." Albert sounded disappointed. "Dad used to get upset when I interrupted his business calls. I guess I'd better ask him later."

"In the meantime, you can help me."

"Aw, Christina, I want to explore," Albert complained.

"First, unpack your suitcase. We'll be here for a couple of weeks. You'll have plenty of time to explore everything."

"Oh, all right." Albert gave in with poor grace. "Where is it?"

"I put it in one of the empty guest rooms. If you don't like that room, choose another, but don't go into the bedroom at the end of the hall. That one is Jace's."

"Christina, do you think Jace is ever going to pitch again?" Albert fell into step beside her.

"Does it matter?"

"Of course it matters." Albert sounded outraged. "Jace is the best pitcher in the majors. He's got to get better."

"But he'll be exactly the same person whether or not he ever pitches again. In fact, he—" Christina stopped in surprise as they rounded the side of the barn and came upon the biggest vegetable garden she'd ever seen.

"Gosh." Albert looked around in awe. "Jace's garden is even bigger than yours, Christina. But yours is prettier. Jace doesn't have any flowers, just veggies."

"Somehow, 'just veggies' seems a rather tame description of all this stuff." Christina fingered a bright red tomato, then moved deeper into the garden to study a short row of sugar snap peas growing under the mesh screens. She wondered if this garden was a result of Jace's interest or if it had been planted by the man who took care of things while Jace was away. Probably the latter, she decided, since Jace's busy schedule could hardly include time for home gardening on this scale. She shook off a vague feeling of disappointment, telling herself it was irrelevant whether or not Jace shared her passion for growing things. But it would have been nice to have been able to discuss gardening with someone who was really interested instead of merely being polite, she thought wistfully.

"Hey, Christina," Albert called from deeper in the garden. "Look at this. Jace's got those miniature watermelons like you grow. Do you suppose we could have one tonight?"

"I don't see why not. Let's go back to the house and get a container to hold what we pick."

After a quick check of the contents of the refrigerator, Christina decided to prepare a Chinese stir-fry dish that would allow her to keep the cooking of the magnificent vegetables to a minimum.

And they were magnificent. She smiled in pleasurable anticipation as she dumped the sugar snap peas into the browned beef and carefully stirred the mixture. She glanced at the microwave as the timer went off to warn her that the rice was done. At least, she hoped it was done. Unfortunately, while the kitchen itself was a cook's dream—large, airy and full of light, no one seemed to have bothered to fill the cabinets with anything more than the most basic cooking utensils, and a minimum of those. She not only hadn't been able to find a wok, but a covered saucepan to cook the rice had proved equally elusive.

Apparently, when Jace stayed here, his meals were limited to frozen dinners.

Ah, well, she thought as she gave the peas another stir in the undersized frying pan, being careful not to spill them. It was only for a couple of weeks. She'd make do.

Her body instinctively tensed as she heard the sound of Jace's uneven tread, and she turned, her eyes skimming over his face. To her relief, he looked slightly better than he had when they'd arrived. His color had improved, the deep lines beside his mouth were gone, and his eyes gleamed with life.

"Have a seat." Christina motioned toward the round oak table set in the bay window. "There's fresh coffee."

"Thanks. Dinner smells…" He frowned as he noticed the bright green of the peas. Moving closer, he peered over her shoulder into the frying pan. "Those look like sugar snap peas," he said slowly. "In fact—" his voice hardened perceptibly "—those look like *my* sugar snap peas."

"There's enough for everyone," she assured him.

"You picked *my* peas!" His voice rose on the strength of his outrage.

"Oh, come on. I've heard of gardeners being possessive about what they raise, but there's no need for you to carry it to extremes. I also picked six ears of sweet corn, four tomatoes and two of your bush melons." She decided he might as well know the full extent of her perfidy.

"To hell with the rest. It's the peas I'm worried about," Jace roared.

"Personally, I'm more worried about your sanity. Have you always been this attached to your peas?" Really, she thought in exasperation, the man was impossible. All this fuss over a few peas.

"Tell me," he bit out, "is it too much to hope that you left a few on the vine."

"Yes."

"Yes, you left a few?" He looked hopeful.

"Yes, it's too much to hope for."

"Dammit, woman!" he yelled. "Do you have any idea what you've done?"

"No." Christina stirred the mixture. "But, unfortunately, I can see you're dying to tell me."

"Don't be flip with me!"

"I'd like to flip you right out the door. Tell you what, I'll stop being flip if you stop acting like the lead in an old-time melodrama."

"Melodrama!" Jace glared at her.

"Bad melodrama. I expect you to start twirling your mustache and present me with an eviction notice any second now."

"I haven't got a mustache and if you stayed in Boston where you belonged—"

"Then poor Albert wouldn't have gotten any supper. I didn't notice you doing anything about it."

"The freezer's filled with TV dinners."

"Wrong, buddy. The freezer's filled with the beginnings of hypertension and high cholesterol. TV dinners on a regular basis are terrible for your heart—something you ought to consider. You're not getting any younger, you know," she added maliciously.

"If you don't keep your grubby mitts off my garden, you're the one who's not going to get any older because I'm going to murder you. And do you know what a jury of my peers will say?"

"The only place you'll find twelve of your peers is in a mental institution!" Christina lost her temper. It had been a long, worrisome day, and she was tired and hot and hungry. And instead of this Neanderthal appreciating her efforts to let him rest while she prepared a meal and settled Albert in, he was carrying on like a certifiable nut.

"Tell you what, buddy." Christina flung the spatula onto the counter, spattering drops of brown sauce over the immaculate cream tiles. "Since you don't like my cooking, you can damn well do it yourself."

"It's not your cooking I object to," he yelled back. "It's what you're cooking."

"So you've said. What the hell is so special about a lousy bunch of peas?"

"Those peas are the result of years of crossbreeding. They were to be seed for next year, and what did they wind up as? Pot luck." He gestured angrily toward the pan.

"There's nothing lucky about them," Christina muttered, her attention caught by the forceful movement of his hands. They were large hands. Powerful hands. She shivered suddenly.

"Thanks to you, I've lost a whole year's work!"

"Wait a minute." Christina suddenly realized exactly what he was saying. "That huge garden you have is an experimental garden? You grow test plants for someone?"

"I grow test plants for myself," he snapped. "I've been studying plant breeding in the off-season at Cal-Davis for over ten years now."

"Cal-Davis?" She frowned, trying to integrate the image of Jace the botanist with her initial impression of him as a playboy athlete. Her imagination wasn't equal to the task.

"The University of California at Davis," he elaborated. "There are some good schools in the West, you know."

"Not for manners. Or common sense," she added. "Didn't it occur to you that simply telling me what you were up to in that garden would have protected your peas?"

"If I'd thought that a guest in my home would feel free to help herself, I would have."

"Well, pardon me," she snapped. "Now that you've reminded me of my position, I'll let you finish dinner, since guests don't cook." With a final, angry nod, she flounced out of the kitchen.

The blasted man, she fumed. How was she supposed to know he was a budding Luther Burbank? No one had ever told her. She stalked into her bedroom and slammed the door behind her. Flinging herself on the bed, she stared blindly at the ceiling. This was going to be the longest two weeks of her life, and not only that, she wasn't even going to be able to give in to the impulse to ignore Jace, because of Albert. He'd never understand her snubbing his hero. It would only confuse and upset the boy, and he most assuredly did not need any further upsets in his life right now.

Christina frowned at the hesitant knock on her bedroom door. Assuming it was Albert back from his exploration of the field behind the barn, she rearranged her angry features into a welcoming smile and called, "Come in."

Her face snapped back to its original expression when the door opened to reveal Jace.

"What do you want?" she demanded belligerently. "Have you thought up some more abuse to heap on me?"

"I brought you a cup of coffee." He carefully limped across the room and set the steaming cup on the bedside table.

Her breath caught when his denim-clad hip brushed against her thigh as he sat down on the bed beside her, but she refused to scoot away like a frightened teenager. She was a mature woman, she reminded herself, well able to handle one man. Especially one as infuriating as Jason McCormick. She tried to whip up her anger to counteract his insidious attraction.

"I was upset earlier," he offered.

"I noticed," Christina said wryly.

"Yes, well..." He ran his fingers through his thick brown hair, creating an endearingly disheveled look that made her long to brush it back. "It was just the shock of it," he said. "Seeing you standing over the corpses like that."

"Tell me, do you also write bad melodramas?"

"I don't write anything. If God had meant man to write, he wouldn't have invented the tape recorder."

"I refuse to get into a theological discussion." She swallowed uneasily as the warmth in the pit of her stomach began to spread upward, affecting her breathing.

"At any rate, I guess I shouldn't have said anything about you picking my peas. You probably don't know any better."

Christina raised her eyebrows at his words. If he thought that constituted an apology, he had another think coming!

Jace stared at her as if trying to gauge her reaction. When she remained silent, he leaned over and kissed her. Taken by surprise at his unexpected move, she opened her mouth to protest. It was a mistake. His lips softened and his tongue surged inside.

Christina stiffened at the intimacy, her hands instinctively moving to push him away. But the moment her fingers touched his shoulders, she was consumed by a desire to pull him closer. To pull him down to her so that she could feel the hard imprint of his body stretched over hers.

Slowly her fingers flexed, kneading the truly impressive swell of his muscles. She offered no resistance when he cupped her chin in his callused palm and tipped her head back to give him better access to her mouth.

She arched upward, pressing against his chest. But much too soon for her growing sense of involvement, he straightened.

Christina stared up into the tiny sparkling lights reflected in his dark eyes and struggled to contain her erratic breathing. It was only a kiss, she told herself. Just a simple kiss. But her emotions recognized that statement for the lie it was. There was nothing simple about that kiss. It had been jam-packed with complex issues—not the least of which was why she had responded the way she had. What was it about Jace McCormick that allowed him to so effortlessly tap into a level of sensuality she hadn't even realized she possessed?

"Why did you do that?" Some of her feelings of uncertainty showed briefly.

"My mother always said to kiss and make up after a quarrel." He gave her an innocent smile that sat very oddly with the knowing gleam in his eyes.

"Someday we must have a long talk about your mother's precepts," she said, embarrassment over her uninhibited response making her voice stiff.

"Don't tell me you're going to turn out to be one of those people who hold a grudge?" He shook his head in mock dismay. "I apologized for yelling at you. What more do you want?"

What more? His words echoed through her mind to be followed by a mental image of Jace leaning over her, his bare chest liberally covered with the same dark hair that covered his muscular forearms. Stop that, she pulled her wayward imagination up short.

"For starters, I'd like an apology that's sincere," she said primly.

"Mea culpa, mea culpa, mea maxima culpa!" He smote his chest in remorse, and Christina was unable to totally suppress the giggle that bubbled out.

"There. I knew you weren't the sort to hold grudges." He eyed her with satisfaction. "Now will you please finish dinner? I took the corpses off the burner."

"If you don't quit referring to those peas as corpses, I'm going to bury them, not cook them."

"Surely I'm allowed to mourn a year's work?"

"I may not hold grudges, but I'm not so sure about you," she said in exasperation.

"All right." Jace stood up and Christina was suddenly filled with a sense of loss.

"I won't mention the peas again. And I would appreciate it if you'd finish dinner." He held out a hand to help her off the bed.

Christina felt his strong fingers close around hers with an easy strength that imparted a feeling of security. A feeling she immediately rejected. Jason McCormick represented a threat to her, not security.

"Tomorrow, I'll ask the lady who comes in to clean, if she'd be willing to take over the cooking," he offered.

"That's not necessary." Christina followed him out of the room, being careful not to brush up against him. His balance was still precarious, she tried to tell herself, but she knew it wasn't Jace's equilibrium she was worried about. It was her own.

"I'd be happy to fix the meals while we're here."

"You!" Jace looked at her as if she'd just confessed a desire to become an exotic dancer. "You never do at home."

Christina held on to her temper with an effort. He couldn't have made his opinion of her as an idle wastrel any clearer if he'd spoken the words aloud.

"I never cook at home for two reasons," she said tightly. "For one, I normally work from eight in the morning to six at night, and then at least two evenings a week I'm out speaking about the needs of various community organizations to various social and civic groups. I simply don't have the time to clean and cook."

"But that's all volunteer work," Jace protested.

"So where's it written that if money doesn't change hands, you aren't really working?" Christina said in irritation at his shortsightedness. "Do you really think that I should demand payment from a bunch of charitable organizations for my work, even though I don't need the money and they don't have it to spare?''

"No, of course not." Jace admitted. "But you said two reasons. What's the second?"

"My housekeeper's been with the family longer than I have," she said ruefully. "You can hardly expect me to fire her so that I can prove I can do her job."

"No." Jace stood aside to let her enter the kitchen. "I guess I never considered the ramifications of noblesse oblige before."

"I strongly suggest you consider the ramifications of a runaway mouth before you wind up with a burnt offering for dinner," she said tartly.

He held up his hands in defeat. "Let me try again. I accept your gracious offer to fix the meals."

"Thank you. I'll—'' She broke off as the kitchen door was flung open and Albert raced into the room, followed by a grubby little boy who looked to be about Albert's age.

"Good afternoon," Christina greeted the pair. They ignored her.

"See, I told you he was here," Albert spoke to the other boy. "Jace, this is Ryan. I found him out by the barn."

"Glad to meet you." Jace shook Ryan's hand, seeming not to notice its dirt-encrusted state and then nodded toward Christina. "And this is Albert's other cousin, Miss Hollowell."

"'Lo, ma'am," Ryan threw in her general direction, as if afraid that Jace would disappear if he took his eyes off him.

Christina swallowed a sigh. Honestly, if she stayed around Jace much longer, she'd begin to think she was invisible.

"Jace is my cousin," Albert bragged.

"Yup." Jace's lips twitched. "Albert is my favorite cousin."

"Jace is my favorite man cousin, but Christina's my favorite woman cousin." Albert's words warmed Christina's heart.

"You, my friend, have the makings of a great diplomat." Christina brushed back a wayward strand of Albert's fair hair. "Would Ryan like to stay for dinner?"

"I can't." Ryan heaved a huge sigh. "We're going to my grandma's."

"You could stop by tomorrow," Albert suggested with seeming nonchalance, but Christina could see the longing in his eyes. Poor lamb, she thought compassionately. How wrong Howard had been in his casual dismissal of her longstanding concern over Albert's lack of friends. Albert wasn't a loner as his father had claimed. He was simply lonely.

"I wish I could, but my mom, she's takin' me and my sisters to Indianapolis to buy school clothes. It starts on Monday, you know," Ryan said.

"This Monday?" Christina frowned. "But it's still August."

"Yeah," Ryan agreed in tones of deep disgust. "They made the school year longer. What grade you going to be in, Albert?"

"I'm on an individualized learning track, second level," Albert muttered.

"Oh?" Ryan stared blankly at him. "I'm going to be in the fourth grade. But it don't matter none. School's school. On Saturday I could come over, and maybe I could bring my baseball glove?" He offered hopefully.

"That'd be great," Albert enthused. "My cousin'll give us some tips."

"Your cousin has an infected leg," Christina reminded Albert.

"Really?" Ryan's eyes widened as he stared at Jace's brace. "Are they going to cut it off? Can I see it if'n they do?"

"The only thing that's going to get cut off is this conversation," Christina replied when Jace simply stared at the little boy in fascinated horror. "It's almost supper time. Albert, why don't you walk Ryan to the end of the driveway and then come back and set the table."

"Aw, Christina," Albert said in disgust, "I'll bet Ryan doesn't have to set the table."

"Nope," Ryan promptly agreed. "I got three sisters. They set the table. I gotta clean out the manure from the chicken coops."

"Oh?" Albert looked taken aback.

"You want some chicken manure for your garden, ma'am?"

"No, thanks." Christina refused. "The nitrogen content's too high. It might burn the plants. Do you have any horse manure instead?"

"Naw, you can't eat horses."

"One would hope not," Jace said dryly. "You two run along and we'll see you on Saturday, Ryan."

"Yes, sir." Ryan ducked his head and scurried out with Albert right behind him.

"Where'd you learn about the nitrogen content of chicken manure?" Jack asked curiously.

"I read it somewhere."

"You garden?"

"Uh-huh." She put the pan back on the burner. "But certainly not on the level you do. What's your specific area of interest?"

"Developing space-saving varieties of vegetables."

"Do you work alone?" she asked curiously.

"Mostly, although I keep in close touch with several plant breeders at Davis. Occasionally I'll test seeds for them here at the farm so that they can see how the plants perform under different conditions. I'm fortunate in that I'm able to work at my plant breeding without having to worry about making enough money at it to pay the bills."

"But if you aren't getting paid for it, how can it really be work?" She eyed him significantly.

"You wouldn't be one of those women who likes to say I told you so, would you?"

"No, I'm not one of those *people* who likes to say I told you so."

"That's a load off my mind." He sank down onto one of the kitchen chairs and absently began to rub his thigh above his injured knee.

Christina surreptitiously watched him, but she held her tongue. Telling him to rest wasn't going to help. What she needed was to figure out a way to keep him off his feet without being obvious about it. A flush stained her cheeks as, unbidden, the image of Jace lying sprawled naked across a bed popped into her mind. Hastily banishing the thought, she forced her mind into more mundane channels.

"You never did get a cup of coffee." She poured him a cup and set it in front of him. "Drink that while I—"

She paused as the melodious sound of chimes filled the air. "The front door?" She looked at Jace.

"Yes. I'll get it." He started to rise.

"No, I will." She put a hand on his shoulder and gently pushed him back down. Her fingers seemed to instinctively cling to his warm skin.

"Yes, nanny," Jace's dry tones broke into her intense absorption and she jerked her hand back.

"And don't you forget it," she said with mock severity. "We wouldn't want them to have to cut off your leg, would we?"

"Little ghoul," Jace muttered as Christina, in response to the second chime, hurried to answer the door.

She could see an overweight, middle-aged woman and a much younger man through the glass window beside the heavy oak door. Christina swallowed a grimace of annoyance. Honestly, of all the times to pick to call on someone, the dinner hour on the day of their arrival wasn't it. But Jace wouldn't thank her if she alienated his neighbors by intimating that she found their manners wanting, she reminded herself.

Opening the door, she said, "Good evening, may I help you?"

"We're here to see Jace McCormick." The woman marched past the astounded Christina into the living room. "Come on, Daryl," she ordered the young man who had hung behind.

"Madam," Christina clipped out, "if you'd care to give me your name and phone number, I'll see that Mr. McCormick gets it."

"We want to see him now," the woman demanded. "We know he's here. One of the women in my office is Ed's aunt and Ed said he was due in today. The Ed who keeps an eye on this place for Jace when he's gone," she elaborated at Christina's blank look.

"And did Ed also tell you that Jace has just gotten out of the hospital and he's here to recuperate?" Christina forced a reasonable tone.

"We won't take long. Now where is he?" The woman looked around the living room as if Jace might be found under the coffee table.

"I'm here." Jace suddenly appeared in the doorway. "But I must admit to being confused as to who you are and what brings you here."

"I'm Iona Fulbrook and this is my boy, Daryl." She gestured toward the inarticulate teenager behind her. "He pitches and we want you to get him a contract with the Lancers."

"I'm sorry, Mrs. Fulbrook, but I don't do the Lancers' hiring. However, I would be glad to drop a line to one of their talent scouts, and tell him about Daryl's pitching."

"They'd give him a contract if you asked them to," the woman insisted. "Everybody knows you're the best pitcher in baseball."

"A title I earned," Jace said shortly. "Now, if you don't want to take me up on my offer, why don't you call any of the three major league teams in the tri-state area and ask them when they have open tryouts. That's a good way for a youngster to break in."

"We did that already and the fools said my Daryl's not major-league caliber. All he needs is a chance to prove himself," the woman insisted stridently.

"Perhaps you should consider sending him to college and letting him play there for four years. That would give him time to develop."

"Waste four years when he could be earning big bucks?" The woman seemed outraged.

"It's your decision. Now if you'll excuse me, we were about to eat." Jace nodded toward the front door.

"Just who do you think you are?" the woman sputtered at his clear dismissal. "Why if it wasn't for fans like me, you wouldn't even have a job!"

"But he'd have his dinner," Christina inserted, wondering at Jace's continued calm. The fiasco with the peas had shown her quite clearly that beneath his normally good-humored exterior lurked a very nasty temper. So why wasn't he losing it with this obnoxious woman?

"Come on, Daryl." The woman swept out of the room only to pause in the doorway and demand, "Don't you forget to call that Lancers scout."

"Whew." Christina closed the door behind the pair with a decided bang. "She was unbelievable."

"I've run into worse." Jace grimaced. "And one'll get you ten, the poor kid has very little talent."

"Poor kid, indeed. I couldn't decide whether he was dumb with embarrassment or simply dumb. Ah, well, Daryl and his career are not our concern. I just hope that the blabbermouth who's broadcasting your arrival doesn't sic anyone else on us."

"Never mind them. I'm starved. Let's go eat." He threw a companionable arm over her shoulders and gave her a gentle tug toward the kitchen.

Christina went, for once oblivious to his nearness. She was still too angry at the sheer gall of Iona Fulbrook. She had no right to invade Jace's home and privacy. Simply because he was a well-known sports figure didn't give her the right to hound him.

Four

___

"Christina, lookit me!" Albert tumbled out of the car Jace was driving, the instant it stopped.

"Careful." Christina smiled at his barely contained excitement, wondering why a simple visit to Jace's therapist should have caused such excitement. Granted, Jace's leg had improved by leaps and bounds over the past few days, but somehow she doubted that that was the cause of Albert's glee. She glanced at Jace for a clue to what had happened, but he seemed intent on locating something in the glove compartment.

Christina's eyes narrowed at the sight of Jace's stiffly held body. As if he were in pain. Or bracing himself for an argument? Her instinct for disaster sparked to life. What had Jace done on his trip to the local hospital that would make him wary of her reaction? She frowned. Offhand, she couldn't think of a single thing. The possibilities for either illicit or immoral behavior in the small rural town were virtually nil. Unless... Her heart sank. Could he have asked Albert to come live with him? Could that account for the boy's excitement?

"Don't you like it?" Albert demanded. "It's just like the one Ryan had on."

Christina hastily refocused her attention and asked, "Like what, honey?"

"My muscle shirt. I got some new clothes like Ryan wears while Jace was at the hospital. I bought them all by myself. But Jace did give me the money," he added fairly.

"What a good idea," she said sincerely, noting the sight of his ribs clearly outlined beneath his skin. A moment of intense sadness engulfed her as her mind unexpectedly supplied the sound of Elizabeth's soft voice lamenting her inability to fatten Albert up. Resolutely she banished it.

"It certainly does show off your muscles," Christina praised extravagantly. "Especially the ones in your arms."

"I haven't got very many." He frowned worriedly at his barely visible biceps.

"They'll grow." Jace handed him a small sack. "If you like, we can start you out on a bodybuilding program."

"Will I look like you?" Albert eyed Jace's broad muscular chest longingly. A longing that momentarily found an echo in Christina.

"It doesn't matter what you look like on the outside. It's what's inside that counts," she assured Albert.

"Maybe," he said dubiously, "but I'd rather have muscles. When can I start weight lifting, Jace?"

"I said bodybuilding, not weight lifting. Weight lifting's not a good idea for someone your age. Let's discuss it in the house where it's cool."

And away from any awkward questions I might ask, Christina wondered, not quite able to shake the feeling that Jace was hiding something from her. But what? Unless her

first fear had been the right one? She eyed Albert thoughtfully as she followed him into the kitchen. Surely if Jace had
asked him to live with him permanently, Albert would be
exhibiting some feeling of sadness at leaving her. Not that
she wanted to send him on a guilt trip. All she wanted was
what was best for Albert's long-term interests, and she
didn't think that living with Jace was. Even if he was turning out to be a whole lot more than the hedonistic playboy
she'd originally thought him to be.

"Have some of the cookies I made this morning, Albert." She gestured toward the racks of cooling cookies on
the counter.

"I love chocolate chip cookies." Albert shoved one in his
mouth.

"Slow down." Christina poured him a glass of milk. "It's
rude to gobble your food."

"But understandable." Jace chuckled as he reached for
a cookie. "These look delicious. You are definitely a person of hidden talents." His eyes roamed slowly over her.

Christina blinked as a wave of heat seemed to flow over
her skin at the hunger she saw mirrored in his dark eyes.

Whoa, girl, she pulled herself up short. You're allowing
yourself to be sidetracked.

Resolutely she turned back to Albert. "What else did you
do this morning?" she asked.

"Well..." Albert slowly reached for another cookie,
clearly uncomfortable with the question. "Jace said he'd tell
you—"

"Later," Jace finished for him.

"Now," Christina said succinctly.

"Oh, it isn't any big deal," Albert said around another
mouthful of cookie. "We just enrolled me in school after
Jace's visit to his therapist. And the principal said I could be

in the same room as Ryan." Albert's ecstatic expression gave
lie to his casual words.

Christina shot Jace a furious look. Of all the underhanded, sneaky stunts for him to pull.

"Albert." Christina tried to keep her seething anger out
of her voice. "You do remember that we're only visiting here
for a while, don't you? Even Jace doesn't really live here. He
lives in Los Angeles."

"Actually, I consider the farm my home," Jace threw in.

"Oh? So you do consider some things?" She gave him an
acid smile. "And here I thought you simply acted on impulse without thinking about the consequences."

"Christina, are you mad at me?" Albert looked confused.

"Absolutely not. I'm simply worried that you might not
understand the situation. None of us, and that includes
Jace, will be here in a few weeks. You and I will be back in
Boston and Jace will be doing what he does best, flinging a
little white ball around."

"I know," Albert said, "but why can't I go to school
while I'm here? All the guys'll be in school. It'll be fun."

"Maybe it would at that." Christina gave in to the plead-
ing in his thin little face. God knows, poor Albert hadn't
had much fun in his life in recent weeks. If only this new
school didn't turn out to be just one more disappointment.

"Thanks, Christina." Albert bounded up out of the chair,
his good humor restored. "Can I go tell Ryan that I'll be in
his classroom?"

"Sure. Just be home by twelve-thirty for lunch."

Christina waited until the door had slammed behind the
little boy and then turned to Jace.

"You egotistical, overbearing, shortsighted—"

"Now, just a minute—"

"Why?" Christina asked seethingly. "Do you have another dirty trick up your sleeve?"

"That was not a dirty trick."

"A dirty, underhanded trick," Christina insisted. "You know we're only here for a couple of weeks. You also know that Albert is under a lot of stress, and yet you deliberately set him up for still more. And for what? To score points off me."

"Believe it or not, lady, you weren't my primary consideration," Jace snapped.

"No, getting your own way no matter who gets hurt was," Christina yelled, and to her mortification burst into tears.

"Christina!" Jace sounded horrified. "Don't cry."

"Then don't do things that make me cry." She ineffectually rubbed her cheeks with the back of her hand. She was so tired of trying to cope with impossible situations. And now she had this overgrown athlete thoughtlessly making a mockery of her efforts on Albert's behalf.

"Sssh, calm down, Christina." Jace's arms closed comfortingly around her, and he pulled her close, tucking her head into his neck.

The raspy texture of his chin scraped over her forehead, and she was overwhelmed by a sense of his strength and his masculinity. Instinctively she snuggled closer, fitting her soft curves into his hard frame. Albert was right, Christina thought dreamily, Jace did have a great body.

The subtle fragrance of his sun-warmed skin drifted into her nostrils, making her excruciatingly aware of him as a physical being. It was not an awareness she welcomed. There was no future in it. On the contrary, it represented trouble with a capital *T*.

"Poor Christina." Jace rubbed her slender back and she arched into his caressing hand.

"If only I knew what was the right thing to do," she inadvertently spoke her thoughts aloud.

"Listen to my mother, of course." Jace's chuckle expanded his chest, pressing against her soft breasts.

"That's right, you mentioned your mother once before." She tilted her head up to look at him. "And here I was thinking you were hatched. What does your mother have..." She paused as she suddenly remembered just when he had mentioned his mother. Her moment of awareness came too late, as his lips closed over hers.

Christina's eyes slowly slid shut as the warmth from his lips sapped her resistance. His hands cupped her soft hips, lifting her more fully into the hardening muscles of his thighs. The evidence of his susceptibility ricocheted through her, heightening her response to him.

She reached her arms around his neck and threaded her fingers through his dark hair. It was soft and silky to the touch and she pressed closer.

Jace tipped her head back and began to cover her flushed fate with soft, lingering kisses.

A languorous warmth was building in her, swamping her normal sense of caution so that when she felt his hand slip beneath her top and splay across her rib cage, she was oblivious to everything but the feel of his burning warmth. She wanted more, much more than the kisses they were sharing. And they were being shared, she thought in satisfaction as the cadence of his quickened breathing echoed in her mind.

The sudden clatter of what sounded like a small army filled her ears at the same time that a feeling of emptiness filled her body as Jace hastily stepped away from her. Christina swallowed, trying to control the thousands of sensitized nerves that were throbbing through her body. The more rational part of her mind might agree that it would be better if Albert didn't catch them kissing, but on some elemental level she was hurt that Jace was so eager to hide their embrace.

"Christina, Christina!" Albert burst into the kitchen, so caught up with his own concerns that he entirely missed the room's explosive atmosphere.

"Good Lord, what's that?" Christina blinked at the sight of the huge furry animal in his arms.

"A rabbit, ma'am." Ryan slipped into the kitchen behind Albert.

"He doesn't look like any rabbit I ever saw." Christina eyed the beast doubtfully. "For one thing, he's much too big and for another, what happened to his ear?" She pointed to the animal's left ear, which was only a third the size of the right.

"It's a genetic flaw." Ryan shook his head mournfully. "Means we can't breed him."

"Poor rabbit." Jace said in a soft-voice aside, and was pleased with Christina's flushed reaction.

Ryan shrugged. "He's only fit to eat."

"Eat!" Christina stared at him in horror. "You're going to eat the Easter bunny?"

"My dad, he raises rabbits for meat. Pity about Jasper though. I kind of like him, but Dad says he's going to be dinner tonight."

"Christina, you got to do something," Albert begged. "They can't eat him. Jasper does tricks."

Jasper shook his head as if in agreement and fixed a beady black eye on her.

"Rabbits can be trained to use a litter box just like a cat," Jace offered thoughtfully.

Great, Christina thought. Just what she needed. A free-roaming rabbit who was bigger than half the dog world. But even though she could foresee all kinds of potential disasters, she was totally unable to resist the appeal in either Albert's or Jasper's eyes.

"If you're willing to train him and if you'll give him a bath first and if Ryan's father will sell him to us, then I guess it's okay," she finally said.

"Oh, Christina, I will. Jasper'll be a perfect pet. Won't you, Jasper?" Albert hugged the large animal. "Ryan, do you think your father'll sell him to me?"

"Sure." Ryan shrugged. "He raises 'em to sell. We'll just eat someone else tonight."

Christina shuddered at his prosaic attitude. "I think we are getting a little too close to the source of the food chain for comfort," she said.

"Life on the farm's like that," Jace said. "That's why I don't raise animals. Come on, boys. I'll go with you to talk to Ryan's father."

"While you do that, I'll run into town and pick up some Kitty Litter and stop by the vet's to find out how to take care of a rabbit."

"Thanks, Christina." The happy grin on Albert's face was more than ample reward for what she was sure would be an endless amount of trouble.

But Jasper turned out to be an ideal pet. By the end of the weekend, he'd mastered the use of the litter box and was given free run of the house. A privilege he did nothing to abuse. In fact, Christina was beginning to wonder why pet rabbits weren't much more common.

"Would you like me to drive you over to the school this morning, since it's your first day?" Christina offered as she handed Albert his lunch money.

"Oh, no!" Albert's eyes widened with patent horror. "Only babies get taken to school, and Ryan said I could sit beside him on the bus."

"Oh, well, in that case..." Christina shrugged, still not certain if she approved of Ryan or not. One thing of which she was certain was that Howard would never have allowed Albert to make friends with him. But then, as Jace had repeatedly told her, Howard was dead and this wasn't Boston.

"All set to go, Albert?" As if her thoughts had conjured him up, Jace walked into the kitchen. "Have an acceptable day."

"I will." Albert shoved his lunch money into the pocket of his brand-new jeans, reached under the table to give Jasper a farewell pat and with a hasty goodbye scooted out the door.

"Have an acceptable day?" Christina asked curiously. "Whatever happened to the traditional 'have a good day'?"

"I read a child psychology book that said telling kids to have a good day was a bad idea because if they didn't they felt guilty."

Christina laughed. "That sounds like something a psychiatrist would say. Poor little kid." She watched Albert through the kitchen window as he sprinted across the backyard toward Ryan's house. "Howard would have a fit if he knew about this."

"Howard was a twenty-four karat, gold-plated snob." Jace poured himself a cup of coffee.

"Maybe he was a little overly concerned with background," Christina conceded.

"He was a snob," Jace repeated. "That's not to say he didn't have a lot of good qualities, because he did, but Howard judged you on who you were. Not what you were."

"He married your cousin." Christina felt obligated to defend him.

"Only because she was an incredibly beautiful woman who'd already achieved quite a bit of international recognition as a model."

"I think that's a gross oversimplification, but I refuse to get into another argument with you."

"Ah, come on. Let's argue." Jace's eyes gleamed with devilment.

"Stop that," she muttered, appalled at the unexpected surge of longing that flooded her at the memory of the last argument they'd had and the devastating kiss that had followed it. She simply had to find some way to counter the elusive tug of attraction he exerted, she told herself. If for no other reason than her own sense of pride.

"Well, if you're going to be a spoilsport, I guess I'll work in my garden this morning. Be careful not to let Jasper out of the house. I wouldn't want to accidently poison him."

Christina frowned uncomprehendingly. "How on earth could you do that?"

"I'm going to spray an insecticide on the winter squash to kill the squash borers. They're a real problem this year."

"What!" Christina glared at him. "And you expect us to eat that stuff after you've doused it with poison?"

Jace opened his mouth, but before he could get any words out, she swept on.

"And not only is it highly toxic—"

"Most poisons are," Jace said sardonically.

"But it'll seep into the soil and stay around for years. And years and years."

"You wouldn't by any chance happen to be one of those organic gardening nuts, would you?" He eyed her suspiciously.

"I am not a nut! I am an intelligent, thoughtful conservator of the earth's resources, who realizes that the most expedient way is not always the best way."

"You're an alarmist."

"I am not, and what's more, my methods work just as well as yours."

"Oh, really? And what do you do about squash borers? Talk them out of the stems?" he mocked.

"No, I imagine they're as open to reason as you are." She rummaged in the drawer beside the sink and extracted a razor-sharp paring knife. Taking it and a roll of tape from the counter, she started toward the back door. "Come on, I'll show you what I do about squash borers."

"Hey, wait a minute." Jace hurriedly limped after her. "You aren't going to slice up my squash vines with that knife."

"You don't have to watch if you're going to be squeamish." Christina gave him a saccharine smile.

"Those plants are the result of years of crossbreeding. They aren't for amateurs to play with."

"First of all, I am not an amateur—"

"Oh?" His dark brown eyes began to gleam as they slipped down over the long length of bare leg visible beneath her green linen shorts.

"And, secondly—" she ignored the goose bumps his inspection raised "—I am highly competent."

"You turned out to be surprisingly competent about some things," Jace conceded, "but we aren't talking about some things. We're talking about my plants."

"No, we're talking about your impossibly possessive attitude toward a collection of stems and leaves."

"And squash borers," Jace muttered.

"Tell you what." Christina stopped on the edge of his garden and surveyed the wilted-looking squash plants. "Let's compromise."

"Why should I compromise?" Jace demanded. "It's my farm, my garden, and my squash."

"And your squash borers," she sniped. "I should have realized from the underhanded, sneaky way you went about enrolling Albert in school that you didn't know the meaning of the word *compromise*."

"I know I'm right about Albert being in school," Jace insisted.

"Do you mean to say you believe that as long as a person's convinced they're right, they should act on that conviction, no matter what the other parties involved think?" She lightly tossed the paring knife from hand to hand.

"Of course not." Jace eyed the knife uneasily.

"Oh? Now, let me get this straight. If you think you're right, you can ride roughshod over my feelings, but, if I believe I'm right, I'm supposed to wait for you to agree?"

"All right." Jace shrugged. "Maybe enrolling Albert in school was a little high-handed, but at the time I felt I was justified. I still do."

"I don't see how you can think that. Even if I had agreed to let you have Albert permanently, you still don't live here. You live in California, and not only do you live in California—" her voice rose with the strength of her feelings "—but you're constantly on the road from February to October."

"Lots of baseball players have kids."

"Yeah, and wives to raise those kids while they're out gallivanting around the countryside. You don't have one. Unless you're planning to marry soon." She ignored the hollow feeling the thought engendered, just as she ignored the relief that superseded it at his negative reply.

"The very best thing you can offer Albert is a hired housekeeper," she pointed out.

"You work, too, even if you don't get paid for it," he countered.

"If you'll remember, I took a leave of absence from all my outside responsibilities after the accident."

"And you intend to stay at home permanently and play at being a mother," he asked skeptically.

"No, after the first of the year, depending on how Albert is adjusting, I'll resume some of my daytime activities. Because I am a volunteer, it'll be easy to schedule my hours so that I'm home when Albert gets back from school. And that's a whole lot more than you can do."

"It isn't the amount of time you spend with a kid, it's the quality of the time."

"Within reason," Christina agreed. "But even your reason should tell you that there's a limit to that theory, and being on the road nine months of the year is over the limit."

"I promised Elizabeth if anything ever happened to her I'd take care of Albert," he said doggedly.

Christina bit back her frustration, deciding it would be wisest to bide her time. His comment about Elizabeth made her think that perhaps Mr. Pauling was right. Maybe Jace's desire to get custody of Albert was an emotional decision based on his love for his late cousin. Perhaps Mr. Pauling would also be right about the impulse fading with time. Although it would be a shame if his interest in Albert entirely disappeared, she thought. Jace might not be able to offer Albert a stable home life like she could, but there were many other things he could offer. Jace McCormick was much more than merely a jock. The trick would be to convince him to maintain contact with Albert without having custody.

"You're blowing this thing all out of proportion. And besides, the school isn't that bad," Jace insisted. "You can see for yourself tomorrow."

"What happens tomorrow?" she asked suspiciously.

"The principal said they hold an open house the evening of the second day of school so that the parents can meet their children's teachers."

"Now that should be an education in itself," she murmured. "And speaking of education..." She glanced down at the squash.

"Tell you what," Jace said slowly. "Just to show you that I'm willing to listen to reason, you can try your method. You may mutilate one of my squash vines."

"One! One is not a valid sample of anything."

"Oh, I wouldn't say that." His eyes lit on her soft lips with a disturbing intensity.

Christina felt an answering spark of desire shoot through her. Honestly, Jace McCormick was the most provoking man, the way he kept dragging sex into every argument. But the thing that annoyed her the most was that he was so successful at it.

Forcing herself to concentrate on the problem at hand, she said, "I want half the squash plants."

"Half!"

"Half," she insisted. "I'll be the control group."

"Not while I'm in control! You aren't going to slice up half my vines."

"Spare me the histrionics. You're the one proposing to poison the poor things, as well as the earth, the water and the birds."

"Talk about histrionics. Tell you what, I'll let you have two vines just in case you accidentally kill one."

"Where's your spirit of scientific inquiry?" she countered.

"Oh, for the love of heaven." He ran his fingers through his hair. "You must be a great fund-raiser. You have the persistence of a gnat."

"Backed by the knowledge that I'm right."

"You aren't right, and I'll prove it. I'll let you have one row of six plants. One," he repeated when she opened her mouth, "and when your method doesn't get results like my spraying will, you'll be quiet about organic gardening."

"One row of squash is not a valid test of a whole system of gardening," Christina protested. "Besides, who knows what atrocities you've already committed on my six plants in the name of chemical gardening."

"That's my offer, take it or leave it."

"I'll take it, but under duress," she grumbled. "I want an outside row and you be careful where you aim your poison."

"I'll wait till you finish your butchering," he said. "Or I might be tempted to exterminate *all* the annoying things in my garden."

"I'd be careful if I were you." She gave him a smug smile. "I'm the one with the knife."

"And the last word." He gave her a reluctant grin.

"Yup." She smiled back, suddenly feeling charitable toward him. He might be terribly misguided when it came to the best way to grow things, but at least he was willing to listen to another viewpoint.

"Exactly what it is you intend to do?" He followed her over to the vines.

"Search the stem till I find a place where it looks like sticky sawdust was put on. That's where a squash borer entered the plant. You simply slit the stem open at that point, extract the worm, and tape the stem shut."

"Very scientific," Jace scoffed.

"I don't know about scientific, but it makes great common sense. The bug's gone and you haven't polluted anything."

"No, but you've shocked the plant's system. You simply don't understand these things," he said with a superiority that infuriated her, but she decided she'd gotten all the concessions she was going to get for one day, so she contented herself with a glare and started to work on her six plants.

"Are you going to wear that to the open house, Christina?" Albert eyed her dubiously.

"What's wrong with it?" Christina glanced down at her white linen suit and blue-green silk blouse. She'd specifically chosen it because the classic cut made it acceptable for almost any occasion.

"Nothing's wrong with it exactly," Albert said uncertainly. "It's just that you don't look like Ryan's mom."

"Thank God." Jace came into the living room in time to hear Albert's words. "In the eight years I've known that woman, I've never seen her out of jeans."

"I should hope not," Christina said under her breath, but Jace heard her and gave her a wicked grin.

Ignoring him, she turned to Albert and said, "One of the first things you learn about life is that people are different. Ryan's mom dresses one way; I dress another. That doesn't mean that one's right and one's wrong, it simply means that we think differently."

"I suppose so, and you do smell better," Albert conceded.

"Thank you." Christina smiled at him. "Now hurry up and change into your suit. We need to leave shortly."

"Suit!" Albert's eyes widened in dismay. "Nobody will be wearing a suit."

"Jace is." Christina nodded at Jace, her eyes running approvingly over the tailored perfection of the three-piece gray suit he was wearing. The crisp white shirt highlighted his deep tan and the muted glow of his garnet silk tie was reflected in his dark eyes.

"I know." Albert sounded disheartened. "I don't suppose you could wear your baseball uniform instead, could you, Jace?" He eyed him hopefully.

"Sorry." Jace ruffled Albert's silky blond hair. "All my uniforms are in my locker back at the stadium in Los Angeles."

"Maybe we could simply stick a baseball in his mouth!" Christina said.

"Now, now, there's no need to be jealous." Jace gave her a smug smile that made her grit her teeth.

"Don't worry, Christina, it's not your fault you're a girl and don't understand the importance of baseball," Albert offered as consolation.

"As far as I'm concerned, the fact that I'm a girl is a thanks giving occasion."

"Definitely." Jace gave her an appraising look that played havoc with her breathing. "And," he turned back to Albert, "I rather like you the way you are, too. I'm sure Christina forgot that this school is a bit different from Walsingham."

"I'll say," Albert agreed emphatically. "I've been here two whole days and no one's said a word about expanding my horizons."

"Albert," Christina responded to the relief in his voice, "do you like Walsingham?"

"I'd like it better if some of the guys liked me, like they do here."

"I see," Christina said slowly, making no attempt to soothe him with a facile lie. Blast Howard anyway, she thought angrily. Why hadn't he taken steps to solve his son's friendless state years ago?

"We've got to hurry," Albert interrupted her thoughts. "Ryan says that if you're late all the good refreshments are gone," Albert said and rushed off toward the car.

But as the evening wore on, Christina was hard-pressed to maintain a pleasant demeanor. For while the school building had been unexceptionable, the same couldn't be said about its inhabitants.

They were greeted upon their arrival by the principal, who fawned all over Jace to the point where Christina was embarrassed for the man. To her surprise, Jace simply ignored it. He was probably used to adulation from some members of the community, she told herself. After all, a town this size wouldn't have had that many celebrities living in it, and some people were bound to overreact to the one they did have.

They finally escaped from the principal only to be waylaid by the gym teacher, who all but begged Jace, in a speech peppered with double negatives, to give his baseball team a few pointers.

Christina gritted her teeth against the man's mutilation of the English language and carefully avoided catching Jace's eye. It would not only be inexcusably rude to laugh at the man, but it wouldn't be very smart. Even though Albert was only going to be here a short time, she wanted it to be happy one, and a teacher who resented him would be a distinct stumbling block to that goal.

The final straw was Albert's teacher. It was as if he were auditioning for the part of the absentminded professor. He greeted Albert with a gentle smile, called him Ryan and told Christina that he'd thoroughly enjoyed teaching her daughter the previous year. The only saving grace as far as Christina was concerned was that he didn't seem to have the slightest idea of who Jace was. He treated him with the same vague courtesy he used with all the parents.

All in all, the evening was not, in Christina's view, a success in any sense of the word. She felt as if she'd knowingly betrayed all of Howard's carefully formulated plans for his son. And complicating things was the undeniable fact that Albert was happy. Christina left the open house, feeling more uncertain than ever.

Five

——

"Do Monday's homework before you go out to play, Albert." Christina slipped a steaming plate of pancakes in front of him.

"But it's Saturday."

"Very good." She nodded approvingly at his indignant little face. "Only nine years old and already you know the days of the week."

"Aw, Christina," Albert moaned. "I can't do it this morning. I got more important things to do. Besides," he hurried on at her skeptical look, "it's not worth it. Like you said, I'm only going to be here for a few weeks, so why go through all the trouble of learning my multiplications tables?"

"And you told me that you wanted to go to this school. So you'll just have to take the bad with the good. Besides, why don't you already know the multiplication tables?"

"Mr. Norell, the headmaster at Walsingham, says that rote learning doesn't accomplish anything. That over the course of the years, I'll learn them naturally," Albert rattled off an obviously oft-repeated dictum.

"By osmosis, no doubt," Jace threw in. "Somehow that doesn't surpise me."

"You're just prejudiced against Walsingham," Christina said, trying to be fair.

"You agree with them?" Jace asked incredulously.

"Actually, no," Christina admitted. "I think the teacher here is right. The multiplication tables should be committed to memory, and the sooner the better." She stared signicantly at Albert.

"But, Christina," Albert wailed, "there's one hundred and forty-four facts. I'll never learn them all."

"Not at one go, although I bet you'll find you already know a lot of them. Why don't we make some flash cards this morning and you can study them in groups of ten."

"Could I do it this afternoon? You see this morning..." Albert stole a sideways glance at Jace and blurted out, "I kind of promised the guys Jace'd come by this morning."

Christina looked from Albert's tense features to Jace's calm ones, her heart wrung with a combination of hope and pity. This seemed an ideal opportunity for Albert to make friends, if only Jace would allow himself to be shown off like a trophy. Hopefully, once the other boys' curiosity about Jace was satisfied, Albert would already be a member of their group. And even if his time here was limited, the practice in making friends would help him once they returned to Boston.

She stared at Jace, willing him to agree.

Jace glanced at her, his dark eyes thoughtfully tracing over her tense features before turning to Albert.

"Where is it that we're supposed to be meeting your friends?"

"At the field over behind the courthouse. The fall soccer league sign-up is today and all the guys play."

"Do you want to sign up?" Christina asked.

"No," Albert replied quickly.

"But..." Christina began, thinking that if the boys all played soccer and Albert played with them, he'd be more a part of the group.

"I can't," Albert insisted. "I'm terrible at sports. I'm always the last one picked when we choose up sides in gym class."

"That's barbaric!" Christina was outraged at the thought of any child standing in the middle of a steadily dwindling group of children until he was alone and the object of ridicule, let alone her beloved Albert.

"It's 'cause I've got two left feet," Albert said sadly. "My gym teacher says either you're coordinated or you're not, and I'm not."

"Nonsense," Jace said briskly. "A great deal of coordination is the result of learned responses. Furthermore, a keen mind can enhance any athletic ability."

"And you certainly have a keen mind," Christina added.

"Yeah, I do," Albert said thoughtfully. "The headmaster said I was a credit to the school when I won that city-wide science fair last spring."

"I could help you after school, and you could get a couple of books from the library on soccer strategy," Jace suggested. "A lot of success in soccer is being in the right place at the right time."

"Would you help?"

"Sure, what's a cousin for?" Jace smiled encouragingly at him.

"I guess I could sign up then." Albert tried to sound nonchalant, but Christina could hear his underlying fear. It would take a lot of courage on Albert's part to lay himself open to ridicule again.

"Sounds like a good idea to me," Christina said briskly. "And you can work on your multiplication tables this evening."

Albert groaned. "If I have to."

"You have to." Jace seconded her words. "Now hurry up and finish those pancakes. We need to leave soon because I have an appointment with my therapist over at the hospital."

"Not that fast," Christina hastily said as Albert tried to shove a quarter of a pancake into his mouth. "Or you'll be the one needing to go to the hospital."

"What does the therapist say about your leg, Jace?" she asked, risking a snub. To her relief, Jace seemed to see nothing unusual about her question.

"That it's coming along by leaps and bounds." His prosaic tone couldn't quite disguise the relief he felt. "The infection's entirely cleaned up, and I'm hoping she'll let me dispense with the brace today. I certainly don't need it anymore."

"She?" Christina instinctively homed in on the relevant word.

"Madge Appleton, my therapist." Jace drained his coffee cup and stood up. "Come on, Albert, I've got to leave now if I'm not going to be late. If you're still hungry, I'll buy you something at McDonald's."

"They'd wait for you." Albert obediently got to his feet.

"Whether they would or not, is not the point. The point is that Madge has other patients to see today, and deliberately messing up her schedule would be both rude and arrogant."

"I guess," Albert said, clearly unconvinced. "Bye, Christina. Can I invite Ryan to lunch?"

"Sure." She watched them leave, pondering Jace's mild rebuke to Albert. What he'd said was absolutely true, but she would have expected that the adulation he received from his fans and the press would have convinced him that his wishes were paramount. It hadn't.

Or was the reason for his desire to be on time this Madge Appleton he'd mentioned? Was he eager to get on her good side? A band seemed to tighten across her chest as her mind insisted on playing an image of Jace lying on a table, a small towel over his hips the only covering while a gorgeous brunette leaned over him, her fingers sensuously probing his firmly muscled flesh.

Stop it, she brought herself up short. It's no business of yours who the man does what with as long as he doesn't directly involve Albert. Besides, Madge is probably fifty-five and plump in the bargain. "Right, Jasper?" Christina reached under her chair and scratched behind the rabbit's misshapen ear.

Jasper shifted slightly in pleasure at the caress, but offered no opinion.

Unfortunately, Madge turned out to be neither middle-aged nor plump, as Christina found out several hours later when she opened the front door to find a gorgeous redhead with a truly memorable figure, who introduced herself as Madge Appleton.

Tinted contacts, Christina thought grumpily as she stared into a stunning pair of jade-green eyes fringed with impossibly long dark lashes.

Christina refused to give in to the impulse to whip off the oversized apron she'd put on when she'd started to bake and gave the woman a determinedly bright smile. "May I help you?" she asked.

"Yes." The woman smiled back, displaying sparkling white teeth. "Is Jace in? He left his brace at the hospital this morning and I thought I'd drop it off for him on my way home."

"He isn't here at the moment. Would you care to wait?" Christina forced herself to offer.

"Perhaps, just for a moment." Madge set the bulky-looking brace on the black lacquered chest just inside the door. "I'm on my way to the Y for a tutoring session with an adult non-reader and I can't be late. Her self-esteem is so low she'd be sure to see it as a personal rejection."

"I know what you mean. I tutored non-readers for years. In fact, I miss it."

"Well, miss no more." Madge laughed. "The Y has a two page waiting list of non-readers hoping for a tutor. I'll give your name to our librarian who coordinates the program."

"Thanks, I think." Christina chuckled as she led the way through the kitchen. "Jace'll be sorry he missed you."

"Don't I just wish. That man's pure fantasy material."

"Yeah, and some of it's a horror film," Christina said dryly. "Would you like a cup of coffee or something cold?"

"Cold, please. The air conditioning in my car conked out yesterday, and I can't afford to get it fixed till payday."

"That's too bad." Christina poured her a large glass of iced tea.

"One of the hazards of the profession," Madge said with a cheerful lack of concern. "Therapists don't make much money, but they do a lot of good. Speaking of jobs, how'd you ever get to be his housekeeper? He's always just used Ed's wife to clean and cook the occasional meal." Madge slipped the question in with seeming casualness.

"I'm not his housekeeper. I'm his guest." Christina decided to tell Madge part of the truth in hope of squelching any gossip her presence may have started. Gossip that might rebound on Albert. "You see, Jace's cousin was married to my cousin and earlier this summer they died in an automobile accident, leaving a little boy. Jace and I are trying to decide on the best way to handle his future."

"That would be the little boy who was at the hospital with Jace this morning. I—" The word came out on a shriek of alarm as Madge jumped to her feet.

Christina blinked, staring at the woman in consternation. What on earth was the matter with her?

"Something bit me!" Madge peered fearfully under the tablecloth.

"Oh, that's just Jasper." Christina reached down and picked him up, cradling him in her arms.

"What is that?" Madge eyed it in disbelief.

"I'm told it's a rabbit."

"I know that! I meant what's it doing under the table?"

"Sleeping, I imagine." Christina shrugged. "When you stop and think about it, there isn't all that much to do under a table."

"Rabbits belong outdoors."

"It's hot outside. Especially for someone wearing a fur coat. Besides, Jasper is litter-box trained."

"He is?" Madge came closer and tentatively patted his head.

"Jace likes him," Christina delivered the telling blow.

"Really?" Madge looked confused. "Somehow I can't picture Jace with a rabbit. Even one that looks like he's got a pituitary problem."

That was because Madge hadn't really gotten to know Jace at all, Christina realized. Jace must have kept their relationship on a strictly professional level, revealing nothing of himself. The knowledge bubbled through her, brightening her spirits.

"It was nice of you to bring Jace's brace by." Christina decided she'd had enough of playing the gracious hostess. "I'm sure Jace will appreciate it." She began to gently sweep Madge toward the door.

Madge, despite her obvious reluctance to leave before she'd sighted her quarry, was no match for Christina's well-honed social skills, and she quickly found herself on the front steps.

"I'll be sure to tell Jace you came by." Christina gave her a warm smile and firmly closed the door behind her.

"Jasper, you and I are going to have to have a long talk about this penchant you have for nibbling on people's ankles. As a method of getting rid of guests it lacks a certain finesse." Christina dropped a quick kiss on his furry head and set him down before returning to her baking in the kitchen.

"Are they gone?"

Christina jumped a foot in the air and whirled around to discover Jace peering into the kitchen from the doorway. "What are you trying to do, scare me to death?" she demanded.

"No, I'm trying to avoid being polite to strangers. I didn't recognize the car out front so I drove past the house and came in the back way and then waited until I heard it drive away."

"It wasn't a stranger." Christina watched him closely, curious about his reaction to the beauteous Madge. "It was your therapist."

"Madge?" He frowned. "What'd she want?"

"You left your brace at the hospital. So she dropped it off on her way home and I offered her a cold drink," Christina said, making no mention of the woman's obvious interest in him. If Jace hadn't noticed, she had no intention of alerting him to the fact. Albert was only going to be here for a little while longer. He deserved the majority of Jace's spare time, which he wouldn't get if Jace began to date, she rationalized.

"That was nice of her," Jace said with a careless lack of interest, "but unnecessary. I didn't forget it. I abandoned it. I don't need it any longer. See." He walked a few steps away from her and then turned, obviously quite pleased with himself. "Now it's simply a matter of doing my exercises. Madge says that my knee is in great shape."

As was the rest of him. Compulsively her eyes lifted from his muscular thighs to linger on the swell of his manhood lovingly cradled in the worn denim of his jeans. Her mouth dried and her breathing shortened with intense longing. She'd never thought of herself as a sensual person, but somehow with Jace she became one. She forced herself to meet his dark gaze. To her relief, he didn't seem to notice her turmoil.

"Speaking of abandonment, where's Albert?" she asked.

"David Blessing, who lives on the road behind us, invited Albert and Ryan to go with him and his father to watch the local boys' high school football team open their season. They'll drop Albert off when it's over."

"You don't have to say 'boys' football,'" she said. "You'd never find a girl dumb enough to stand there and let someone try to mangle her."

"You're just jealous because you're the weaker sex." Jace grinned at her.

"Not mentally." She grinned back. "Are you hungry?"

"Ravenous." His eyes focused on her lips and Christina swallowed uneasily, having the distinct feeling they were talking about two entirely different things.

"I'll get lunch then," she said. "But I want you to know that I appreciate your efforts to help Albert fit into the group."

"Speaking of appreciation, I've been meaning to tell you that I'm glad you invited yourself along."

"Oh?" she said cautiously.

"Uh-huh. I was against your coming in the first place because I was afraid you'd spend all your time moaning about the lack of cultural amenities here at the farm and make Albert dissatisfied with everything. And, instead, you pitched right in and helped out. As a matter of fact, I haven't eaten this well since I left home eighteen years ago."

He really hadn't had much of an opinion of her, Christina thought grimly. Only the fact that her own initial opinion of him didn't bear too close a scrutiny made her keep her angry rejoinder to herself. Instead, she picked the least emotionally charged topic to respond to.

"Why don't you simply hire yourself a housekeeper?"

"Because housekeepers tend to be obtrusive. You aren't. I can talk to you. You're . . ." He gestured impotently with his hand.

Not quite understanding what he meant, but not wanting him to think it mattered much to her, she returned the conversation to its original topic. "Anyway, I really do appreciate your helping Albert."

"Why not thank me in the time-honored way?" His eyes gleamed with devilment. And something else. Something she found much hard to put a name to.

Christina slowly crossed the kitchen, stopping just in front of Jace. She could feel the heat of him, almost as if they were already touching, and the sensation raced along her nerve endings to heighten her awareness of him to a fever pitch. Her body swayed closer to his.

Jace's arm closed around and pulled her against him, making her explicitly aware of his body's reaction to her. She pressed closer to the hardening plane of his body, and the pressure of his mouth increased, parting her lips and allowing his tongue access to the softness within. A tiny moan escaped from her as he filled her mouth and his tongue probed deeply. She caressed his jaw, enjoying the sensual feel of its rough texture as well as the moist softness of his lips. His groan of satisfaction startled here, and reminded her that she shouldn't be kissing Jace McCormick in the first place.

Forcing herself to step back, she stared blindly at his chin while she tried desperately to come up with a topic that would somehow defuse the sexual tension that was humming between them.

"Have you inspected the squash plants lately?" She almost groaned out loud as she heard the inane words. Of all the stupid... She sighed inwardly. The problem was that for some reason all Jace had to do was touch her, to throw her completely out of her normal mode of behavior. It made no sense, but it was undeniably true.

"Squash?" She took heart from the fact that Jace sounded as confused as she felt.

Having no choice but to follow through on her choice of topics, she forced herself to meet his eyes. The sight of the barely restrained passion seething in them did nothing to help her regain her normal equilibrium. Her gaze skittered away, focusing instead on the kitchen cabinet over his left shoulder.

She licked her lips and doggedly continued, "You remember. The squash you were trying to poison. I just wondered if you'd checked the plants today?"

"When would I have done that?" He reached for her again, but Christina, for once obedient to her mind—which was screaming caution—and not to her emotions—which were urging her back into his arms—moved toward the kitchen door.

"Why don't we go have a look at them and then I'll fix some lunch?" she suggested brightly.

"If that's all you're offering." He fell into step beside her.

"When does Albert find out if he made the team?" Christina asked, determined to keep the conversation on neutral grounds.

"They don't choose here. All the kids who sign up are randomly assigned to a team. You know, if he lived with me he could finish the soccer season with his group," Jace suggested with seeming casualness.

"Sure, no doubt with a baby-sitter in the stands as a cheering squad!" Christina said scathingly, all her pent up emotion finding an outlet in anger. "Because you wouldn't be there. You'd be somewhere pitching."

"Only until October and I promised Elizabeth—"

"As you are so fond of telling me, Elizabeth is dead. I, on the other hand, am very much alive and I have no intention of allowing you to drag Albert from pillar to post while you follow a baseball team. Or to leave him here at the farm with a baby-sitter," she continued ruthlessly when he tried to say something. "As far as I'm concerned, the subject is closed."

"The only thing closed is your mind," Jace said in exasperation.

"Oh, I don't know. Your squash plants have quite a few closed leaves." She pointed to the plants in front of them. "It looks to me like your chemicals poisoned more than just the bugs."

"Squash borers are notoriously hard to get rid of," he excused himself, "and besides yours don't look all that much better."

"Yes, they do." She carefully counted. "I only have nineteen wilted leaves, you've got twenty-four."

"But my plants are bigger."

"So they should have rebounded better," she said triumphantly. "Spraying is a bad idea, and that definitely proves it."

"What it proves is that your idea of a scientific experiment is straight out of Disneyland," he said in disgust.

"I know a wilted leaf when I see one," Christina said smugly.

"And I know a complete lack of scientific methodology when I see it," Jace countered. "What we really need is more controls."

"Perhaps," she conceded, "but you should start your study in the spring by removing the moth that lays the egg that becomes the squash borer."

"Unfortunately, spring's a busy time for me. It's all I can do to get the plants into the ground. As it is, I have to depend on the teenager down the road to actually tend them."

"My point precisely." Christina nodded. "You're much too busy for time-consuming things like proper gardening techniques or small boys."

"But not too busy for irascible women." Jace grinned at her.

Christina stiffened. "I wouldn't know. I don't know any irascible women."

"Ha! You are the most illogical—"

"Me! You have the corner on the illogical market. I, on the other hand, am operating from sweet reason."

"Parts of you are definitely sweet." Jace's eyes lingered on her lips and his eyes darkened to deep chocolate. "However, it isn't your thought process. Why is it that organic gardeners are such fanatics?"

"Maybe because you proponents of chemical warfare are so irresponsible."

"It's hardly irresponsible to want to put fresh, unblemished food on people's tables."

"What's wrong with a few blemishes?" Christina countered. "That's half the trouble today. People are trading physical perfection for a host of chemicals doing who knows what to their insides."

"I know what you do to my insides," Jace muttered with an intense glance that sent a quiver of excitement racing through her—until she realized that he could just as easily be referring to what he'd termed her irascible behavior as to her kisses. And she could hardly ask which it was.

"You're probably hungry," she finally said. "Let's go eat. We can discuss your irresponsible use of the land later."

"My irresponsible...!" Jace roared. "We aren't going to discuss any such thing now or later. This land is mine."

"The next line of that song is, 'This land is your land,'" Christina said smugly, stifling a laugh at the audible sound of his teeth grinding in frustration. She didn't really expect to convert him to nonchemical gardening techniques, but if she could just get him thinking about the dangers of overspraying, she'd be satisfied. He really was a very intelligent man. In fact, from what she'd seen of some of his experimental vegetables, he bordered on brilliant. Maybe she should work on him a little more this afternoon.

But to her disappointment, she didn't see much of him that afternoon. Once he'd eaten the lunch that she'd prepared and helped her load the dishwasher—without so much as a hint from her—he'd disappeared into his study. It wasn't until the exuberant sound of Albert returning from his ball game echoed through the house that he emerged.

"I take it the game was a success?" Jace smiled at the excited little boy.

"It was fantastic!" Albert sighed ecstatically. "We won. When I'm in high school, I'm going to play football."

"Oh, no, you're not," Christina objected. "You could get hurt."

"Aw, Christina, everybody plays football," Albert said in disgust.

"Maybe we could work on your kicking game," Jace said before Christina could tell Albert what she thought of that particular argument. "You've got the build to be a great kicker."

"Do you think so?" Albert stuck out his thin little chest in pride.

"Without a doubt."

Christina threw Jace a grateful look. From what she remembered about football, kicking was relatively safe. There were rules against trying to annihilate the kicker.

"What happened to Mr. Blessing?" Christina asked, wanting to thank the man for taking Albert to the game.

"They had to get home for dinner, so he just dropped me off. But David is going to bike over after he eats and work on his soccer game with Jace and me. He's just as bad as I am," Albert said happily.

"An admirable trait in a friend." Christina chuckled. "I take it this morning went well."

"Great. Everyone wanted to meet Jace."

"Marvelous. Now since that's out of the way, suppose you work on your multiplication tables before dinner. I cut flash cards out of poster board earlier and put them on the desk in your room."

"Aw, Christina, I'm too tired now."

"That's a shame," Jace said. "I was looking forward to our soccer practice tonight." He shook his head in pseudo-sympathy.

"But . . ." Albert sputtered.

"If you're too tired to do your homework, you're too tired to play soccer." Jace delivered the thinly veiled ultimatum in a pleasant tone of voice. "It's up to you. Only you know how you actually feel."

"I guess I'm not that tired," Albert conceded. "Oh, I almost forgot, Christina. Mrs. Blessing's going to call you. She was complaining about getting stuck doing the soccer raffle and I told her that you were great at that kind of thing and that you'd help her."

"Thank you for the recommendation," she said dryly. "You'd better go wash. Dinner'll be on the table in about forty minutes."

"I'm not very hungry. We had hot dogs and French fries and potato chips and ice cream and candy bars and soda at the game."

Christina laughed. "I'll serve you a couple of antacid tablets for dinner. Now off you go." She watched him disappear into his bedroom and then turned to follow Jace into his study.

He sank down in his oversized leather chair and eyed her questioningly.

"I want to thank you," she began, determined to find out why he was reinforcing her discipline.

"You did thank me, remember?" His eyes traced the curve of her cheek, then lingered on her lips.

"I was referring to your backing me up on the question of his homework."

"You didn't think I would?" His face hardened and Christina felt an unexpected frisson of fear chase over her skin. Jace would make a formidable enemy, she suddenly realized.

"I don't know you well enough to predict what you'll do, do I? I mean," she continued at his hard-eyed stare, "you want custody of Albert, and indulging his whims would be one way of casting me as the heavy and you as his buddy."

"And it never occurred to you that I might find your views on child raising worth supporting? Maybe I should just behave like the unthinking animal you clearly seem to

DISCOVER FREE BOOKS

&

FREE GIFTS

From Silhouette

S	D	A	V	R	Y	B	X	N	M
G	I	F	T	N	C	A	S	P	Y
Z	D	L	N	B	U	L	T	R	S
R	T	N	H	N	E	F	T	A	T
D	H	I	A	O	V	K	D	M	E
N	W	E	K	H	U	O	W	S	R
O	C	T	M	U	T	E	D	D	Y
I	L	P	F	L	P	B	T	I	E
P	E	A	J	S	M	H	I	T	P
S	E	N	S	A	T	I	O	N	E

As a special introduction to Silhouette Sensation we will send you:

4 FREE SILHOUETTE SENSATIONS
plus a
FREE TEDDY
and
MYSTERY GIFT

when you return this card.

But first - just for fun - see if you can find and circle five hidden words in the puzzle.

THE HIDDEN WORDS ARE:

SILHOUETTE • SENSATION
TEDDY • MYSTERY • GIFT

Now turn over to claim your
**FREE
BOOKS & GIFTS**

FREE BOOKS CERTIFICATE

YES! please send me FREE and without obligation, four specially selected **Silhouette Sensation romances**, together with my FREE **teddy** and **mystery gift**. Please also reserve a Reader Service Subscription for me. If I decide to subscribe, I shall receive 4 superb Sensations every month for just £6.00, post and packing FREE. If I decide not to subscribe, I shall write to you within 10 days. The FREE books and gifts will be mine to keep in any case. I understand that I am under no obligation whatsoever - I can cancel or suspend my subscription at any time simply by writing to you.

FREE TEDDY

MYSTERY GIFT

6SOSS

Mr/Mrs/Miss
(Please write in block capitals)

Address

_____

_____ Postcode _____

Signature _____

I am over the age of 18.

NO STAMP NEEDED

Reader Service
FREEPOST
P.O. Box 236
Croydon
CR9 9EL

believe I am.'' His hand suddenly snaked out, grabbing her arm and tumbling her into his lap. His fingers speared through her hair, holding her head immobile as his mouth closed over hers with ferocious intent. When she parted her lips and allowed him the greater intimacy he demanded, he seemed to restrain himself and began to slowly explore her mouth.

He tasted of coffee. Christina extricated her hand from where it was sandwiched between their bodies and touched his face. The rough texture of his stubbled chin rasped over her sensitive fingertips, causing her skin to tighten into goose bumps. She moaned as she felt his probing hand slip beneath her shirt and press against he soft skin of her stomach. A wash of desire burst over her like a wave, making her twist blindly in his arms.

''You can make me so damned mad, and then I touch you and...'' He sighed and began to lightly nibble on her earlobe.

Christina arched her neck to give him greater access, her breath catching in anticipation as she waited for his hand to move higher. She could feel her breasts swelling with an overpowering need to be touched, and a yearning sound escaped her parted lips.

''You're so soft and warm and sweet smelling. Like a whole field of freesias.'' He nuzzled the soft skin behind her ear. ''I want to touch you everywhere.''

Christina gasped as his hand suddenly closed over her breast and a tightening sensation shafted through her. She pressed blindly against him, and his fingers gently tugged on the roseate tip, leaving it a tight, aching bead of desire. Christina twisted restlessly, the feel of the rigid shape of him pressing against her, heightening her passion. She felt a cool drift of air across her overheated skin as he slowly pulled her top upward to reveal her breasts.

"You're exquisite." His hoarse voice filled her with a sense of exultation that left no room for doubts. All she wanted was to feel. Jace's mouth closed over her breast and his tongue rubbed over the sensitized tip, sending spirals of sensation coiling through her.

"Please," she muttered, blindly clutching his head and holding him tightly against her, "I want—"

"Christina." Albert's thin voice was like a dose of cold water on her fevered emotions. She froze, and although Jace hurriedly pulled her top down over her breasts, his arms tightened when she tried to scoot off his lap.

Swiveling his chair around to face the open doorway, he called out, "We're in my study, Albert."

Hastily Christina arranged her features into what she hoped was a reasonable facsimile of her normal expression.

"Christina—" Albert burst into the room "—can I learn the twos and threes tonight?"

"Why—" Her voice cracked. She firmed it and went on, "Why don't we compromise? You do the twos and nines, and then move on to the threes and eights and so on."

"All right." Albert eyed them speculatively. "Why is Jace cuddling you?"

"Well..." To her embarrassment Christina could feel a blush staining her cheeks.

"Is it his sexual urges?" Albert asked curiously.

"His *what*?" Christina gasped, trying to ignore the way Jace's suppressed laughter was pushing his hard thigh muscles into her soft hips.

"You know. His sexual urges," Albert repeated. "Mr. Taggart gave us a lecture in sex education class last year, and he said that as gentlemen we have to learn to control our sexual urges. But I'm not sure what he meant because the only urges I ever have around girls is when stupid Susan makes fun of me and I have an urge to smash her.''

"Yes...well..." Christina stammered, mentally groping for an explanation. "Jace and I weren't..."

"What Christina means is that she's absolutely exasperating and, since my mom always told me to kiss and make up after an argument, I thought that if I kissed her before we argued, we wouldn't."

His lighthearted explanation chilled her.

"Nothing makes girls more reasonable," Albert said, "although Christina's better than most."

"Thanks for the testimonial," she said tartly, climbing off Jace's lap. She needed time to think. Something she found impossible to do when he was touching her.

"That was a compliment, Christina." Albert eyed her worriedly.

"And I appreciate it." She gave him a quick hug. "But I'd better see about dinner now." She threw a bright, meaningless smile in Jace's general direction and hurried out to the kitchen.

Once there, she leaned up against the counter, took several deep, steadying breaths and tried to make sense of the chaotic state of her emotions. But only one thought surfaced with any degree of clarity. The kiss they'd shared had been nothing more than a lighthearted bit of fun to Jace, while she had found it a mind-blowing experience without precedence in her past.

She was becoming much too involved emotionally with him. And as if that weren't bad enough, she could see no signs of her feelings being reciprocated on any but the most basic level. What had Albert called it? Indulging his sexual urges?

She slammed her hand down on the counter in frustration. Was that all she was to Jace? A handy release? But that made no sense, either. She forced herself to think rationally. Willing women couldn't be that hard for him to find. Even here in Indiana. Madge had followed him home on the flimsiest of excuses.

Unless... She frowned as she thought of something else. Would Jace use her attraction to him to get her to give him custody of Albert? On the surface, it seemed unlikely. But what did she really know about Jace? She had drawn a lot of conclusions during their stay here, but how accurate they were was anyone's guess. It was entirely possible that he was being very careful to present himself in a favorable light. It was also entirely possible that he had kissed her for no other reason than that he'd enjoyed it.

And, maybe she was overreacting. Maybe her best course of action would be to simply let things take their course without taking them so much to heart. If that was possible, she thought ruefully.

Six

_____

Christina, Christina! Guess what?" Albert burst through the front door, dropped his book bag on the hall floor and rushed into the kitchen.

"The house is on fire?" Christina smiled indulgently as the little boy hopped from foot to foot in barely contained excitement.

"I'm a crowd!" He beamed at her.

"Sometimes it seems like it," Christina agreed solemnly.

"No, at school," he said impatiently. "They only chose two fourth graders and I was one. The teacher liked my screams."

"Well, I'd certainly like a more logical progression of your thoughts. Suppose you start again at the beginning, and this time give me a few more facts so that I can properly appreciate the honor that's been done you."

"The senior class always does a fall play. It's a horror show."

"That goes without saying." Christina grinned at him.

He ignored her. "And they needed a crowd of kids to find the body and we all auditioned and Mrs. Obradovich, the English teacher who's directing the play, said I had a truly unforgettable shriek." He smiled in remembrance. "And she said Ryan was a natural and so we're both in it and all the others guys are jealous 'cause we get to get out of class five times to practice."

Albert sat down at the kitchen table, an expression of blissful satisfaction on his thin face.

Christina frowned as the obvious flaw in Albert's news suddenly occurred to her. "When is this play, Albert?"

"The last week in October. Right before Halloween."

"I see."

Christina filled a plate with the molasses cookies she'd made that afternoon, poured a glass of milk and handed them to him while she tried to find the words to remind Albert that they wouldn't be there then. That their time at the farm was definitely drawing to a close. Jace's knee was improving dramatically, and it wouldn't be that much longer before he went back to doing whatever it was that baseball pitchers did, and she and Albert would have no excuse to linger at his home. A feeling of sadness engulfed her as she glanced around the sunny kitchen. She'd miss this place, but most of all she'd miss Jace. Even though he was infuriating at times, there was something about him that fascinated her.

"What's wrong, Christina? You look sad." Albert eyed her worriedly.

Christina sighed, wishing there was a way to soften the blow. Damn, she thought angrily. Why couldn't all this have happened in Boston? Because the Walsingham Country Day School would never produce a horror show where a blood-curdling scream would get you a part, she answered her own question. They'd undoubtedly do something either socially relevant or historically significant.

"I'm sad because I know how much you want to be in the play, and I also know that we're going to be leaving for home pretty soon."

"But that was before I got the part," Albert protested. "We can't leave now. What difference does it make? I've already missed the start of school back in Boston anyway."

"Don't I know it." Christina grimaced at the memory of the acrimonious conversation she'd had with the headmaster of Walsingham, who'd called her decision to remain in the "wilds of the Midwest" academically irresponsible.

"Albert, listen to me." Christina took his small hands in hers. "You knew when we came here that we were just visiting while Jace's knee healed."

"Yes, but—"

"No." Christina shook her head. "No arguments. First, you listen to me. Then I'll listen to you."

"Jace's knee is almost better. He hasn't had to wear his brace for over a week. Pretty soon, his team will activate him, and then he'll leave to join them. We can't stay in his house when he's not here."

She took a deep breath and forced herself to consider Albert's feelings and not her own. "Jace will be living at his home in California when he leaves here. But, if the reason you want to stay is Jace, I'm sure he'd be willing to take you with him and extend your visit so you can get to know him better."

"Without you?" Albert looked at her in horror.

She gave him a rueful smile. "Jace invited me along this time because of you, but we can't expect him to put up with me forever. Things change."

"You mean he might get married?" Albert nodded knowingly.

Christina tried to ignore the pain that lanced through her at the thought of Jace with another woman. It wasn't her business what Jace got up to, she told herself, wondering why her emotions found that so hard to accept. She knew she was becoming much too involved with Jace, but even knowing that, she was unable to stop the question that popped out.

"Has Jace said anything to you about getting married?"

"Not exactly. When he was explaining about sexual urges...you know, he's a lot better at it than Mr. Taggart was."

He's a lot better at it than anyone I ever met, Christina thought dreamily.

"Anyway," Albert continued, "Jace said that when you travel so much it's hard to get to know anyone well enough to want to marry them. But Ryan's oldest sister, the one who's always asking about Jace, says that love can strike in a minute."

"That's lust, not love," Christina said dryly, "and I hope you aren't discussing Jace's private life with anyone."

"Not much." Albert ducked his head guiltily. "It's just that she keeps asking and I have to say something."

"Try saying 'mind your own business.'"

"She'd hit me, but I guess it doesn't matter." Albert sighed. "If we're not going to be here, I'll tell Mrs. Obradovich tomorrow that I can't be in the play."

The sight of his woebegone face tore at Christina's soft heart. "Tell you what, don't say anything for the moment. We don't know exactly when we'll be leaving and, since your role doesn't require much rehearsing, maybe we could simply return for the week of the play."

"Oh, Christina!" Albert threw his arms around her and gave her a breath-stopping hug. "I love you. You're the greatest. Can I go tell Ryan, huh, please?"

"Sure, just be back in time for dinner, and if you fall in his pigsty again, I give you fair warning that you're going to be the one to wash your clothes. By hand. Down at the creek. You hear?" She gave him a level stare, her nose twitching distastefully at the memory of yesterday's disaster.

"It was an accident," Albert defended himself.

"And if it happens again, it'll be *your* accident."

"I'll be careful." Albert grabbed a handful of cookies and rushed out the kitchen door, leaving it open behind him.

Thoughtfully Christina closed it as she considered the situation. Albert wasn't the only one who was becoming involved in things. As Madge had predicted, the librarian had called the next morning and asked her to tutor non-readers a couple afternoons a week while Albert was in school. Mrs. Blessing had also called and Christina had agreed to keep track of the tickets for the raffle the soccer team was holding. But those were insignificant entanglements when compared to her involvement with Jace. She frowned blankly at the kitchen wall. She wasn't sure why or how, but every day that passed bound her a little closer to him. If she had any sense at all, she'd grab Albert and run back to Boston before she got in any deeper.

Ah, well, she sighed. She'd spent her entire adult life being sensible. For once, she intended to follow her instincts and logic be damned.

"What's the matter?"

Christina jumped at the sound of Jace's voice.

"Don't sneak up on people like that!"

"Sneak! That was hardly my 'sneak up on people' approach."

"You could have fooled me."

"Could I?" He eyed her narrowly. "Somehow I doubt that. You're one helluva sharp lady, but that doesn't mean

I'm not game to try. Tell you what, you stand by the sink and look out the window and I'll show my sneak approach."

"Don't be silly."

"Silly?" Jace looked down his nose at her. "I consider my honor has been insulted and I demand satisfaction."

Christina noticed the tiny dancing lights reflected in his eyes and felt a shiver of excitement feather through her. Providing him with satisfaction could be the highlight of her emotional life to date.

Entering into the spirit of things, she went to the sink and, turning her back to him, stared out the window.

"Now, sing something like you usually do when you're working."

"What kind of fool am I?" Christina began, trying to listen for the sound of Jace's sneaker-clad feet on the tiled floor. She didn't hear a thing. The first intimation she had that he was directly behind her was when she felt his warm breath electrifying the hairs on the back of her neck. A second later his arms encircled her, his hands closing over her breasts.

"Jace!" Her voice came out on a startled squeak. "What are you doing?"

"Frightening the wits out of you." He nuzzled the soft skin behind her right ear.

That he was, but not for the reason he thought. Christina swallowed uneasily and tried to move away, but it proved impossible. Jace merely tightened his arms, and her body began to tingle at the pressure.

"Um, listen Jace . . ." She shuddered as he began to trace the curve of her ear with the tip of his tongue. "I'm not frightened."

"You would be if you could read my mind." His chest shook with laughter, and Christina absorbed the variations of his body with a feeling of intense pleasure.

"Good Lord," she whispered in mock horror, "is it your sexual urges again?"

"Somehow, all I have to do is look at you and I'm consumed by the damn things."

"Fancy that." Christina laughed unsteadily as he began to rub his callused palms back and forth across her cotton-covered breasts, creating the most delightful friction.

"No, fancy you." He turned her in his arms and captured her lips with a rough urgency that gave added validity to his words.

Christina opened her mouth, welcoming the pressure of his probing tongue. But to her disappointment, he made no effort to take advantage of her willingness. Instead, after one quick kiss on her parted lips, he lifted his head and, resting his forehead against hers, looked deep into her desire-clouded eyes.

"As a matter of fact, I'm the one who should be frightened out of my wits," he muttered as he stepped away.

"Of me? I'm harmless."

"You're a lot of things, lady, headed by sexy and closely followed by frighteningly competent, but harmless you aren't."

"Why is it that men find competence in a woman frightening?"

"Because men have very fragile egos," he replied promptly, "and they like to think they have an edge on women."

"You mean you actually believe all that sexist hooey about women being the weaker sex?"

"You are."

"Am not."

"Want to wrestle?" He gave her an exaggerated leer and Christina felt her heartbeat speed up.

"This is a ridiculous conversation." She made a valiant effort to restore things to some semblance of normalcy between them. "What was it you wanted?"

"I came in to tell you I wouldn't be here for lunch tomorrow. I just talked to Madge, and she thinks it's time to check in with Methodist Hospital in Indianapolis since they're overseeing my recovery."

Christina felt a chill of fear tighten the skin of her face. "Is something wrong with your knee?"

"On the contrary." Jace reached around her and took a handful of the molasses cookies cooling on the counter. "Madge feels it's completely healed and she wants the hospital to second her judgment."

"Oh." Christina glanced down at the floor, trying to control the maelstrom of confused feelings surging through her. Relief that his knee was healed was all mixed up with sadness that their time here on the farm was almost over. And it wasn't only for Albert's sake that she was reluctant to leave the farm, she admitted honestly. She'd miss Jace, too. Miss the sharp intelligence, his wry sense of humor and their perpetual arguments about the best way to grow things. But most of all she'd miss his physical presence, the touch of his hand and the taste of his mouth.

Perhaps she should tell him about Albert's sudden entrance into the world of the theater and then try to lead him into offering to let her and Albert stay at the farm until after the play was performed in October?

No, she immediately rejected the idea. For one thing, Jace would know as well as she that a member of the crowd didn't require that much rehearsal. That it would be a simple matter for her and Albert to return for the actual performance, and the only reason for them both to stay would be to be closer to Jace—and he wouldn't even be there, he'd be in California. And, finally, the longer they postponed going home to Boston, the harder it would be for Albert to adjust to a new school and for her to forget Jace.

She sighed despondently.

"You aren't pleased?" Jace sounded hurt.

"Of course I'm pleased. I was just thinking about something else." She forced a bright smile.

He gave her a searching glance and then, seeming to accept her words at face value, said, "How about coming along and keeping me company while I take care of the weeds?"

"Sure." Christina happily followed him outside. "I've already pulled the weeds from around my squash."

"Your wilted squash."

"They're not as badly wilted as yours," she countered. "And you've still got weeds."

"I won't for long. I should be able to spray them all this afternoon."

"What!" Christina came to a halt at the edge of the garden and stared at him. "Do you mean to tell me you intend to use a herbicide? On top of all the other poisons you've already dumped on that ground?"

"I have to get rid of the weeds before they rob the plants of nutrients and water," Jace defended himself.

"Have you ever considered simply yanking them out? Not only does it get rid of the weeds, but it doesn't leave a lot of deadly chemicals behind, lying in wait for future generations."

Jace looked at her in annoyance. "Strike intelligent."

"What?"

"From the list of things you are," he elaborated. "Your attitude toward modern farming borders on the irrational."

"And yours borders on being willfully blind."

He ran his fingers through his hair. "Dammit, Christina, use your head. Even if I wanted to break my back trying to hand weed a test area this size, I couldn't. During the baseball season, I'm lucky to be able to squeeze in a few days' visit every three weeks or so."

"So, mulch."

"Mulch?" Jace blinked.

"You know, mulch, ground cover. According to Albert, the attic is loaded with bales of hay."

"No, it isn't." Jace frowned at the sprawling house. "It doesn't even have an attic."

"The barn's attic."

"The barn doesn't have an attic, either." He gave her a superior look. "It has a loft."

"A rose by any other name." She waved her hand dismissingly. "Why don't you use the hay up there to mulch? Not only will it conserve water and keep down the weeds, but over the winter it'll decompose and build up the soil."

Jace rubbed the side of his chin thoughtfully. "Maybe, but spraying would be quicker."

Christina watched the slow movement of his large, powerful fingers. Her breath shortened as she remembered the feel of those fingers on her own face. Telling herself that her timing was bad, she forced herself to concentrate on the subject at hand. For some reason that she didn't want to fully explore, it was becoming increasingly important to her to convert Jace to her own way of thinking about gardening.

"It wouldn't take us very long to weed and spread the straw."

"I can't lift those hay bales," Jace finally blurted out as if ashamed of the fact. "I'm under strict orders not to put any weight on my knee."

"No problem. I'll simply push the bales out of the hole in the attic floor and let them fall to the ground. It'll be safe enough. Albert's at Ryan's, Jasper's in the house and you've got enough sense not to stand underneath."

"Why do I hear an echo of an insult in that compliment?" Jace grinned at her.

"Guilty conscience?" She grinned back. "Come on, let's get busy with the weeding."

As Christina had predicted, with the two of them working together, they made short work of the weeds. She left Jace to finish the last plot of miniature watermelons while she went to the barn to start pushing the hay out of the loft.

It was dusky in the huge loft and Christina looked around, spotting the stacks of baled hay immediately. As she'd thought, it would be a simple matter to shove them across the bare wooden floor and through the hole. Dusting her dirty hands on the back of her denim shorts, she pushed one out the opening. With a cautious look below, she gave the bale a final shove and watched in satisfaction as it hurled downward, hitting the concrete floor with a muffled thump before the thick twine holding it snapped and hay flew everywhere.

"Win some, lose some." Christina turned away from the mess below and began pushing the next bale toward the opening. A garden the size of Jace's would probably take twenty bales she estimated. By the time she'd shoved the needed bales through the opening, she was hot, tired, sweaty and more than ready to escape from the claustrophobic atmosphere of the loft into the cooler barn below. She clattered down the stairs, pulling up the hem of her T-shirt as she went, to allow the slight breeze to cool her overheated skin.

She paused on the last step as she became aware of Jace leaning up against the open barn door, watching her. Her mouth dried at the hot glow in his eyes, and she slowly let her shirt fall, prey to a confusing mixture of emotions. A fragment of her mind was ecstatic that she could produce such a degree of interest in Jace by merely adjusting the length of her shirt, while another fragment was busily shouting a warning. A warning Christina didn't want to hear but couldn't entirely ignore.

"If we load the hay in that oversized garden cart I saw in one of those equipment rooms in the back of the barn, it shouldn't be much of a problem to get it out to the garden," she offered.

"I already brought it out. It's right behind you." To her relief, Jace followed her lead. It was bad enough fighting her own burgeoning feelings without fighting his, too.

She shuffled through the gigantic pile of loose hay and, picking up an armful, tossed it into the cart. It was hot prickly work, and if the alternative hadn't been to let Jace loose with his poisons, she would have suggested they leave it until later.

"Drat!" she muttered as she tripped over one of the pieces of twine that had held the bales together and pitched forward. Jace lunged for her, missed, and they both tumbled into the three-foot layer of loose straw.

"Look at the bright side," Jace said at her expression. "If you'd gotten clumsy up in the loft, you could have fallen out of the opening and splattered your brains all over the barn floor."

"What an elegant turn of phrase you have."

"I know a mess when I see one," Jace defended himself.

"I'll say." She stared significantly at him. "You look like you're auditioning for the part of the scarecrow in *The Wizard of Oz*. You've got straw stuck everywhere." She pulled a golden stem out of his dark brown hair. The silky strands of his hair brushed lightly across her fingertips, making her long to run her fingers through it.

"I feel like it, too." Jace sat up and yanked his T-shirt over his head and tossed it aside. "It prickles."

"Oh?" Christina's voice came out on a breathless squeak as she stared in mesmerized fascination at his bare torso. Tiny bits of honey-beige straw dotted the thick brown hair that covered his chest and arrowed down to disappear into the waistband of his jeans. A compulsion to touch him washed over her, the intensity of which would have frightened her if she hadn't been so enmeshed in her response. Blindly she reached out, tracing over the bits and pieces of straw. "It makes a pattern," she said dreamily.

"Yes, the pattern's definitely beginning to clear," Jace said cryptically. He captured her wandering hand and pressed her palm to his chest, trapping it against his hot damp skin. The crisp texture of his body hair curled against her palm, sending shivers of awareness darting up her arms. She closed her eyes, the better to concentrate on the sensation, and her own heartbeat sped up as if trying to adjust itself to the increasing rhythm of his. The scent of the straw added a musky, elemental aroma to the air around them, totally in keeping with the primitive slant of her feelings. As if drawn by an invisible cord, she leaned toward him, her gaze locked longingly on his slightly parted lips.

"Christina? What are you guys doing?" Albert's curious voice hit her overheated emotions with the force of an icy gale. Sighing, she twisted around to see Albert and Ryan standing in the barn's huge open double doors, staring at them.

"That kid's timing is appalling," Jace bit out, letting go of her hand after one last squeeze.

Or a godsend, Christina told herself. In another minute, she'd have been kissing Jace, with no thought to such mundane considerations as the fact that they were clearly visible to anyone walking by the open barn door.

"I'm helping Jace mulch." Christina got to her knees.

"How do you mulch?" Albert came into the barn, followed by the curious Ryan.

"Well, first you find a great big weed—" Christina gave Jace a mischievous grin "—then you cover it up. Like this." She grabbed an armful of straw, dumped it on Jace's head and then jumped to her feet.

Unfortunately, she didn't reckon on Jace's superb coordination. His hand closed over her ankle and he jerked her back against him.

Her bottom brushed against his hard thighs, momentarily disorienting her. It was all the advantage he needed. He began to toss straw onto her.

"Now, some weeds need a particularly thick blanket of straw." He accompanied the advice with a huge armful of straw on her head.

"You rat. I'll never get this stuff out of my hair," she wailed.

"You started it." Jace threw more straw on her.

"Black plastic works better." Ryan's judgmental voice stopped Jace in midthrow.

"What?" Jace turned to the grubby little boy.

"Plastic works better'n straw."

"It's not biodegradable," Christina took advantage of Jace's momentary distraction to scramble to her feet.

"It only comes in black," Ryan said. "Not in colors."

Christina opened her mouth to explain what biodegradable meant and then decided this wasn't the best time. "You're probably right, Ryan. Why don't you and Albert give us a hand with this?" She cautiously maneuvered the cart between her and Jace. He still had a gleam in his eye that she mistrusted.

"You want us to help carry *all* that straw to the garden and stand in the scorching sun while we spread it around?" Albert suddenly assumed the downtrodden expression of a victim of child labor.

"Yeah, that's what we want, all right," Jace replied with a cheerful lack of sympathy.

"But it's so hot, and—" Albert broke off as Ryan nudged him and then whispered something in his ear.

Albert nodded, turned back to them and said, "What's it worth to you?"

"What's it worth?" Christina eyed him in disbelief.

"In money," Albert clarified.

"We're your family and you're trying to hold us up?" Christina was outraged.

"A laborer's worth his hire. It says so right in the *Bible*," Ryan pronounced.

"It's the law of supply and demand," Albert elaborated. "Like we studied in economics last year. You got a big supply of straw—"

"And I'm about to demand some help," she shot back.

"You're absolutely right, boys," Jace broke into the argument. "A laborer is worth his hire. What do you think you're worth?"

Christina frowned at him, but he ignored her as he watched the two boys hold a whispered consulation.

Finally Albert said, "Ten dollars apiece."

"Fair enough." Jace nodded. "And, when we're finished, I should have some time to help you with your soccer if you like."

"Yeah!" Albert exclaimed while Ryan nodded enthusiastically.

"Now what do you suppose would be fair compensation for my coaching services?"

"Compensation?" Albert asked warily.

"Uh-huh. Let me think. I vaguely remember some sports writer saying I was being paid almost fourteen thousand dollars an inning, and an inning takes about ten minutes or so. So I usually earn about fourteen hundred a minute." Jace beamed out at them. "However, coaching's not as hard as pitching. So shall we say five hundred an hour?"

Christina swallowed hard to keep from laughing at the sight of the boys' stunned faces. She waited while they held a whispered consulation, and then Albert said, "Actually, we'd be glad to help with the hay for free."

"That's nice of you boys," Jace said.

"Well, we ain't stupid," Ryan grumbled.

"But it really isn't fair," Albert insisted. "You told me if I wanted money I should earn it, and then, when I try to, you get nasty."

"My dad, he pays me to weed," Ryan threw in helpfully.

"You do have a valid point," Christina agreed. "But it wasn't the money I minded. It was the way you responded to a request for help by trying to extort money from me."

"What's the difference?" Albert looked confused.

"It's an ethical consideration," Jace said.

"Oh, a grown-up thing," Ryan said dismissively. "Us kids ain't got no money, we can't afford them ethy things."

"Tell you what, Albert, how about if I post a list of jobs and what I'm willing to pay for them on the refrigerator door?" Christina offered.

"And in the meantime we can go out for ice cream after practice tonight," Jace suggested.

"What kind of ice cream?" Albert asked cagily.

"Any kind you want," Jace replied promptly.

"As long as you don't get sick," Christina said.

"It's a deal." Albert beamed happily and he and Ryan began to throw straw into the cart.

Christina followed suit, well pleased at the way Jace had managed to make the boys happy while still not giving in to their attempt to take advantage of the situation. He'd make a marvelous father. She paused as in her mind she saw the image of a sturdy little dark-haired toddler dragging a baseball bat behind him.

"The heat getting to you?" Jace rubbed the back of his hand across her flushed cheek.

No, but you are, Christina thought dreamily, savoring the sensation of his roughened knuckles brushing across her soft skin.

"Christina?" His voice sharpened.

"I'm fine."

"You don't look it. You look a little fuzzy. You aren't used to the heat of an Indiana summer. Why don't you go get us all some cold drinks while the boys and I lay the straw?"

"Yeah, farmin's man's work," Ryan stated.

Christina eyed him narrowly as she debated whether or not to squash his incipient male chauvanism. It was Albert's worried expression that decided her. After all, Ryan wasn't her responsibility. Albert was, and Albert already knew better than to make such knee-jerk statements. His mother had seen to that.

"In that case, I'll see to the drinks." She smiled reassuringly at Albert and started toward the house, relieved to be escaping from the sun for a few moments. Jace was definitely right. She wasn't used to this kind of intense heat.

Seven

Christina heard the front door open and, a second later, Jace's deep voice yelling, "Christina, where are you?"

"In the kitchen," she yelled back, trying to analyze the tone of his voice. Did it contain joy or despair? Had the news from the hospital in Indianapolis been good or bad?

Reaching for a towel, she dried her hands and pasted a smile on her face. She'd spent a miserable day while he'd been gone. Her feelings had seesawed between a sincere wish that the hospital would give him a clean bill of health and an equally sincere, if irrational, wish that they'd tell him that he had to continue his therapy for a few more weeks. For she knew that a physically fit Jace would rejoin his team and she and Albert would fly home to Boston.

She glanced around the sunny kitchen. In some strange way this house seemed more like home than the house she'd lived in all her life. It's just because you're more directly involved in taking care of it, she tried to tell herself, wishing it really was as simple as that.

"There you are." Jace came into the kitchen, and one look at his face was sufficient to tell her that his news was good. His eyes positively glowed with excitement.

"I'm me again," he announced.

"Oh, and who were you before?" Christina couldn't resist his infectious gaiety.

"Less than a man."

"Nonsense, you aren't measured by your knee." Involuntarily her eyes strayed, and a slight warmth stained her cheeks.

"Why, Christina Hollowell! Was that a sexist look you just gave me?" He chuckled. "And here I thought you liked me for my mind."

"So give me the specifics about what the doctor said." She hurriedly changed the subject.

"That I'm one hundred percent and can do anything I could do before. I called the Lancers' front office from the hospital, and I'm joining the team in Cincinnati just as soon as I can get there."

"How nice." Christina turned back to the cake she'd been icing, trying not to let her hurt show. All it had taken was the mention of baseball, and he was off without even a token show of regret at leaving them. At least it proved she was right about one thing, she thought grimly. Jace should not be Albert's guardian.

"Actually, that part of it is." He paused as if weighing his words. "The front office is chartering a plane to fly me to Cincinatti," he finally said.

"I hope you have a safe trip." Her voice sounded overly hearty to her sensitive ears. "Albert will be sorry not to have been able to say goodbye."

"I intend to stop by his school on my way to the airport. Besides, I'll see him on Saturday."

"How so?" Christina looked at him, confused at his words.

"When you drive over to Cincinnati to see me pitch. Burt, the team's manager," he elaborated at her blank look, "is going to let me start on Saturday. So don't be late. As long as it's been since I last pitched, I might get knocked out of the box in the first inning."

"Nonsense," Christina automatically responded to his worried expression. "After a three-week rest you'll be fresh. The batters are the ones who'll be tired."

"Hmm." His face brightened at her logic. "Well, now that that's settled, I'd better pack."

"Just a minute there." Christina stopped him as he started to leave. "Nothing is settled. First of all, Albert and I will be in Boston this weekend, not—"

"Boston!" Jace glared at her. "What the hell are you going to Boston for?"

"We live there, remember? We only came to Indiana on a visit."

"Which isn't over," Jace insisted. "Christina, you can't leave now. Not yet. Albert's settling in so nicely at school, and I don't even know if I'll be able to pitch. I could be right back here on the farm on Monday. And besides—" he gave her a calculating look "—you wouldn't desert all those poor defenseless plants in the garden, would you? They need you."

But what about you, she wondered. Do you need me? On the surface, it certainly didn't seem so. It appeared to her that all he really wanted was to rejoin his team. But on the other hand, he must honestly want them to stay, because she'd just offered to leave and he'd emphatically rejected the idea. On some level, at least, he did want her. Or did he simply want Albert, and she was a convenient means to keep the boy here?

Christina thoughtfully chewed her lower lip. There was no way to tell and she could hardly ask. It would make her sound incredibly immature. Even if that was the way Jace made her feel sometimes.

"I guess we could stay a while longer." She ignored the voice of reason that was trying to tell her that the longer she stayed, the harder it would be to eventually leave.

"Good. I'll leave the tickets for your seats at the main ticket office. And I'll lay out a route for you before I go. Not that you'll have any trouble. Cincinatti's only about a hundred miles or so from Indianapolis and it's all expressway."

"I won't have a problem. I have a great sense of direction," she assured him, when what she really wanted to do was to ask just where she fitted into his future plans. If, indeed, she did. The thought that she might not, kept her silent.

"I'll go pack."

"Fine." Christina resolutely turned back to her cake, trying not to let her uncertainty show. She was loading the dishwasher when a bellow from Jace's bedroom drifted into the kitchen.

"Honestly! Men!" she muttered as she went to find out what had happened.

"What's the matter?" She pushed open the half-closed door to his room. "Did you..." The words died in her throat as she saw Jace standing in the middle of the room holding one end of an elastic bandage. The other end was wrapped around his knee. Apart from a miniscule pair of black briefs, which barely covered him, it was all he wore.

Her eyes skimmed over his broad shoulders, lingering along the thick muscles of his chest before falling to study the flat plane of his stomach. The same dark hair that covered his chest and arms was also liberally sprinkled over his firmly muscled thighs and calves. Christina drew in a shaky breath and tried to ignore the aching sensation growing in the pit of her stomach.

"What was it you wanted, Jace?" She made a monumental effort to sound like the sophisticated woman she knew herself to be.

"Help. I dropped the metal clasp that holds the bandage together and, if I let go to search for it, I'll have to rewrap the bandage. Would you mind getting the piece?" He gave her a hopeful look. "I think it fell under the bed."

"No problem." She walked over to the king-sized bed and bent down to peer beneath it. It was hard to see in the dim light, and she groped for the metal clasp.

"You know you really have the nicest shaped tush of any woman I've ever seen," Jace said reflectively.

"What?" Christina jerked up and smacked her head against the bed frame. Rubbing her throbbing skull, she looked at Jace in disbelief and demanded, "What did you say?"

"I said—"

"Never mind." She thought better of having him repeat it. "I heard you."

"Then why did you ask?"

"Because I simply didn't believe *what* I heard."

"You mean no one's ever complimented your cute little tush?"

"No! And you shouldn't, either."

"Why not?" He gave her an innocent look she didn't trust for a second.

"Don't give me that wide-eyed-boy-down-on-the-farm look. You know perfectly well that one simply doesn't say things like that in our culture. Good Lord, how would you

like it if I were to start making personal comments about..."
She gestured toward his briefs.

"Go ahead, I wouldn't mind." He grinned at her. "I think honesty is by far the best policy."

"This conversation isn't honest, it's outrageous," she grumbled, "and you *know* it."

"All I know is that I like the shape of your tush," he said stubbornly.

Giving up, she stuck her head back under the bed and hastily located the clasp he was looking for. She straightened up and held it out to him.

"Fasten it for me, would you? If I try to do it while I'm bent over, it won't fit right."

Put like that, there was no gracious way to refuse. Christina slowly made her way across what seemed like acres of cinnamon-colored carpeting. She knelt in front of him, her downcast eyes focused on his feet. He had nice feet, she noticed approvingly. Big, with well-formed toes.

"The end attaches behind my knee." Jace's voice sounded deeper than usual to her sensitive ears. She raised her head, her eyes skimming over the hardening planes of his body. An intense wave of desire rippled through her, which for once she made no effort to control. Instead, she let it radiate through her, sensitizing her and making her vitally aware of him. Jace was about to leave, and she didn't know when, if ever, she'd have the opportunity to touch him again.

Tentatively she touched the skin above the bandage and leaned closer as she adjusted the clasp, breathing deeply of the scent of soap and masculine cologne that clung to him. Her hand inched up the back of his thigh. The wiry texture of his hair tickled her palm, setting her heart to pounding in slow, heavy strokes.

"Christina!" he said hoarsely. His response gave her the courage to look up and her eyes caught at the sight of his arousal. A totally unexpected feeling of power shuddered through her at the knowledge of his vulnerability to her. It cut through all her self-doubts and uncertainties. The wonder of the sensation rocked her back on her heels and she stared up at Jace in bemusement.

His eyes were closed and his long lashes were dark against his tanned skin. His lips were slightly parted and she could hear his breath whistling through them. The brilliant afternoon sunlight streaming in through the floor to ceiling windows engulfed him in a golden aureole of light, as if he were a luminescent being from another world. But he wasn't, she thought with unexpected possessiveness. Jace was real. Here. Now. But not here for long. Soon he'd be leaving. The knowledge acted as a spur and she leaned down and dropped a kiss on his ankle, then began to slowly, very slowly, place kisses in a serpentine pattern up his leg. Jace's body was totally rigid by the time she reached his upper thigh, his harsh breathing giving mute testimony to his growing desire. Daringly she slipped her hand inside his briefs.

His reaction was instantaneous. Reaching down, he pulled her up and she quivered as her warm skin rubbed against his.

"You're irresistible," he said roughly. His fingers brushed back the soft curls from her flushed cheeks, pushing them behind her ears. "Your hair is like corn silk—soft, golden and clinging." He studied the bright curl encircling his deeply tanned finger, then moved his hand to her neck. Christina shuddered as a band seemed to tighten around her chest, restricting her breathing. Slowly, his fingers caressed her nape, exploring the sensitive skin behind her ears and her eyes began to close.

"No! No," he repeated more softly. "Don't close your eyes. I want to watch them as I kiss you. Do you know that they turn almost black when I make love to you?"

A moment of paralyzing shyness gripped her and her eyes flew to his, but the absorbed expression on Jace's face reassured her.

She touched his upper arms, her fingers flexing against the smooth texture of his skin to probe the heavy muscles beneath. Intensely curious about him, her fingers danced over his shoulders and she explored the slight hollow at the base of his neck. Leaning forward, she lightly licked the indentation with the tip of her tongue. A salty taste flooded her mouth and she was surrounded by the warm musky scent of his body.

Christina dropped another kiss on the corner of his mouth and the rough-silk texture of his freshly shaven skin rasped across her soft lips. A sigh of satisfaction escaped her as a powerful shudder ripped through him and he pulled her closer. A tingling sensation shot through her breasts at the contact.

His fingers speared through her hair, tipping her head back, and his mouth took hers.

Christina's lips parted and she eagerly met his thrusting tongue. Excitement exploded in her, heating her skin and setting her heart to racing.

Jace spread his legs slightly and, grasping her hips, pulled her up against him.

Christina squirmed closer. She ached for him. Ached with a bone deep need that left no room for doubts.

"I can't stand much more of this, Christina." Jace swept her up in his arms.

"Be careful of your knee!" Some lingering vestige of sanity made her protest.

"To hell with my knee," he ground out. "You're all that matters." He laid her on the bed and followed her down.

She wound her arms around his neck and pulled him close, wiggling at the feel of him on top of her.

"Don't do that." He hastily lifted himself on one elbow. "I'm damn close to losing what little control I do have...." His eyes seemed focused on some inner vision, the pupils dilated with the force of the emotions raging through him.

Wonderingly, Christina caressed his cheek. Jace turned his head and his tongue darted out to taste her skin.

She shivered at the sensations overloading her nerve endings. A melting warmth was flowing from his body, rendering her boneless.

She stared up at him with heavy lidded eyes, willing him to make love to her, but unable to put her demand into words. She watched helplessly as he reached into the bedside table drawer and pulled out a tiny silver foil packet. He turned back to her, freezing as he caught sight of the pale flesh visible between her cotton shirt and her jeans.

The skin on her abdomen began to flutter under the force of his heated gaze and a rising sense of excitement spiraled through her. Her breath escaped on a jagged sigh as he leaned over and began to nuzzle the exposed skin.

Christina gasped as he suddenly yanked her cotton shirt over her head and tossed it onto the floor, baring her breasts to his searching eyes. "You're incredibly beautiful!" He lowered his head and, catching one tight pink nipple between his teeth, gently rubbed the tip of his tongue over its pebbly hardness.

Christina's fingers bit into his shoulders as a burning hunger fired her senses. "Jace!"

"And don't you forget it," he muttered, placing soft kisses down the slope of her breast and across her rib cage until his progress was impeded by the waistband of her jeans. With meticulous care he unzipped them and pulled them downward, his mouth following.

Christina grabbed for his head, intent only on stopping the slow torture. She couldn't stand this anymore. She wanted to feel the heavy weight of his body covering her, to feel the heat of him deep within her.

"Jace! Stop playing games." She lifted her hips as he pulled her jeans down over her legs.

"I've never been more serious in my life." His deep tones had the ring of a vow, but Christina was too caught up in her own response to notice. All she could feel was a desperate sense of heated urgency that burned away inhibitions.

Jace nudged her legs apart and slid between her thighs. He grasped her hips and then slipped his hands beneath them to lift her to him. With a powerful surge, he filled her. Christina shivered as the shock waves of his possession eddied through her.

"Christina," Jace's voice seemed to be coming to her from a great distance. She forced her eyes open and blinked to clear her vision. His features were sharply etched by the desire gripping him, the cords on his neck stood out in stark relief against his tanned skin and the muscles on his shoulders were bunched. He looked like a man caught in the grip of an intolerable tension. A rising sense of exhaltation filled her as she realized that she had done this. She, Christina Hollowell, had driven this sophisticated man to the point where nothing else mattered but her. For one moment out of time, she was his whole world. The only person who had any meaning for him.

"I'm afraid I'm not going to be able to hold on much longer." He surged forward, intensifying the pleasure she was experiencing almost past bearing.

She wrapped her long legs around his hips, intent on satisfying the coil of tension that his provocative movement was tightening. His rhythm was agonizingly slow, exquisitely pleasureable. Finally, when her need had reached the point where she felt as if she were about to shatter into a million tiny pieces, Jace increased the pace, sending her hurtling into a magical world of pure sensation.

Slowly she drifted down through the soft, cushioning clouds of languor that had effectively protected her from reality. Reality in the form of Jace's bright brown eyes gleaming down at her.

She forced herself to meet his gaze when what she really wanted to do was to hide, to burrow under the covers and pretend this had never happened. It shouldn't have. If she'd been displaying even a fraction of her normal common sense, she would have fastened his bandage and beat a hasty retreat. The problem was that she never did seem to behave normally around Jace, she thought ruefully. There was something about him that seemed to short-circuit her normal sense of self-preservation. But even knowing that what had happened could cause complications, she couldn't regret it. For the first time in her life she truly understood what all the fuss was about. In Jace's arms her womanhood had found a definition that she hadn't realized was possible and she couldn't regret that. No matter what the eventual cost. A sudden fear lanced through her at the thought of losing what she'd just found.

She shivered and the movement sent a lingering ember of passion through her as her breasts touched against his hair-roughened chest.

"Sorry, darling. Am I too heavy?" Jace dropped a quick kiss on her nose as he levered himself off her.

"No," she answered absently, much more interested in his endearment. He'd never called her darling before, so why now? Because they'd made love and he felt she expected it, or because he actually meant it?

"Thank you, Christina," Jace brushed the backs of his knuckles across her softly flushed cheeks. "That was—"

"Your bandage has come undone." Christina hastily tried to redirect the conversation. She couldn't bear listening to him rationalizing what had happened or worse, thanking her for a good time.

"Christina, I have to—" he began doggedly.

"Get to Cincinnati." She rolled off the bed and began grabbing up her scattered clothing.

"The fastener for your bandage is on the floor," she threw over her shoulder as she practically ran from the room, ignoring his clipped expletive at her retreat.

She didn't care, she thought as she scurried into her own bedroom, stark naked, her arms full of clothes and snapped the door closed behind her. Nothing mattered but that she have a few minutes alone to regain her composure before she faced him again.

And there was no doubt she'd lost it. She grimaced as she pulled on her clothes. The minute she'd touched him and he'd begun to kiss her, she'd forgotten everything. Who she was. Where she was. What she was. The massive problems making love with Jace could cause. None of that had mattered. All that mattered was that he continued to make love to her. She'd had no idea that it was possible to lose oneself in another person to that extent. To feel anything so intensely that you didn't care if the world stopped, as long as he didn't.

But what had Jace felt, she wondered as she picked up her brush and began to restore some semblance of order to her tousled curls. She closed her eyes and tried to remember, but specifics eluded her. All she had were impressions of heat, pressure and extreme pleasure. She had a vague memory of his muffled cry of satisfaction, but that was all.

Was it possible he hadn't found the experience as incredible as she had? That he wasn't as attracted to her as she was to him? But then why make love to her? Because of Albert? Could his making love to her have been a ploy on his part to get her to agree to his guardianship of Albert?

No, she immediately rejected the idea. Jace could be aggravating in the extreme, but he had a bone-deep basic integrity. He wouldn't stoop to seducing her to get her to agree to something. Not that he'd actually seduced her, she admitted with her usual lack of self-deception. He might have invited her into his bedroom, but she'd made the first move toward him.

Christina tossed her hairbrush down on the dresser in disgust. Things would have been much simpler if Jace had turned out to be the brash, insensitive egomaniac she'd originally thought he was. She would have found that Jace McCormick easy to deal with. Unfortunately, the real man was proving much more difficult to handle. But she'd do it. She had too much pride not to at least try.

It was that same sense of pride that drove her out of her room to say goodbye to Jace before he left. It was vitally important to her that he not realize just how deeply his lovemaking had affected her.

But she found her chosen role of unflustered sophisticate difficult to maintain when Jace, for some reason she didn't understand, seemed determined to discuss what had happened between them. But by the simple expedient of finding urgent business elsewhere whenever he tried to talk, he was finally forced to leave with the subject untouched. Although what good he thought discussing things was going to do, she didn't know, Christina thought as she watched him climb into the cab.

Unless, perhaps, Jace was serious and felt obliged to ask her to marry him. Could he really be that old-fashioned? A piercing surge of excitement filled her at the thought of being married to Jace, before it faded in the clear, cold light of logic. No one was *that* old-fashioned, and besides, fantastic sex was not sufficient reason for marriage.

But that wasn't all they had, an insidious little voice in her mind whispered. They had the same sense of humor, the same sense of community involvement, the same love of growing things and the same ideas on raising children.

Sure, and if she was to somehow coerce him into marrying her, she would spend the next ten years or so being a grass widow while he flitted around the countryside with his baseball team. She tried to put the reins on her imagination up short. No, she would be crazy to get involved any further with him. What happened this afternoon was a fluke and couldn't be allowed to happen again.

Resolutely she turned away from the window as the cab disappeared down the road. Now that Jace was actually gone, it would be easy to put him into perspective, she assured herself.

She was wrong. Jace refused to be relegated to the back of her mind. There were reminders of him everywhere. And to make matters worse, Albert moped around the house, mourning Jace's departure and calculating to the exact minute when they could leave for Cincinnati to see him again.

Christina bit back an urge to snap at the boy, mainly because she felt exactly the same way. To her growing unease, she found that she missed Jace more with each passing day, not less. Her disquiet was made worse by Jace's nightly phone calls. To her hypersensitive ears, he sounded stilted, and she couldn't help but wonder if he was regretting what had happened between them.

By Saturday she was so excited about actually seeing Jace again that she found herself grinning inanely at the mirror as she brushed her teeth. Fortunately for her overwrought nerves, the trip to Cincinnati proved uneventful, and she and Albert arrived at the ballpark with time to spare.

Christina collected their tickets from a busy clerk behind the ticket window and, firmly clutching Albert's hand, made their way into the stadium.

Albert looked around eagerly. "Can I get a pennant, huh, please, Christina?"

"Later. First, I want to find out where our seats are. Let's find an usher and ask."

"There's one there." Albert headed toward him and Christina hurried after him.

The bored-looking usher suddenly assumed a respectful demeanor when he looked at the ticket stubs she showed him. "You're right behind the visitor's dugout, ma'am." He lead them to their seats. "Front row."

"Rats!" Albert leaned over the rail and peered out at the acres of sparkling green grass.

"What's the matter? These are great seats." Christina looked around with interest.

"I should have brought my glove. I'll bet I could have caught a foul ball in this seat."

Christina frowned. "Foul ball?"

"Yeah, the batters hit lots of foul balls into the stands, and as close as we are, I'll bet lots of them'll go by."

Oh, great, Christina thought ruefully. Smething to look forward to. Getting bashed in the head. She glanced longingly out at the center field bleachers. Out there they'd have been safe. But here she had clear view of the pitcher's mound, she reminded herself. And of Jace. She felt a shiver of excitement as she allowed herself to dwell on the thought of actually seeing Jace again.

"Don't you just love baseball games, Christina?" Albert bounced on his seat in excitement.

"No," she said honestly. "Ball games are not my thing."

"Don't worry," Albert consoled her. "It's because you're a woman. Mom hated them, too, and Dad used to say she couldn't help it, because women didn't have the right kind of genes. So Dad and I would go to see the Sox ourselves."

Christina smiled at him, inordinately pleased at the way he'd been able to talk about his parents without the paralyzing grief he'd felt before they'd come to Indiana with Jace. At least their visit had done wonders for Albert's emotions, even if it had made a mess of her own.

"I take it you're a Red Sox fan?" she asked him.

"Of course, I am." Albert looked at her in astonishment. "They're the best team in the majors, but that's the American league. This is the National league. The Lancers have a shot at the Western division title, you know."

"No, I didn't," Christina said, inwardly amused at his serious expression. "You'll have to tell me—" She broke off as the Reds took the field to the screaming approval of the approximately fifty thousand fans.

Christina looked around the packed stadium consideringly. "You know, Albert, I'm beginning to appreciate how the early Christians must have felt at the Coliseum. Lancer fans seem to be at a premium around here."

"We'll just have to yell louder." Albert suited his words with action as the first Lancer stepped into the batter's box.

Christina glared at the dugout's overhanging roof in frustration. It was impossible to see inside, and her need to at least catch a glimpse of Jace was fast escalating into an intolerable compulsion. She found being so close and yet so far away frustrating in the extreme.

But when Jace finally did make his appearance, it didn't satisfy her need. The man who purposefully strode to the pitcher's mound looked like Jace, but then again he didn't. There was no humor in his dark brown eyes and no smile on his tightly compressed lips. His entire attention was focused on the batter. It was as if the universe consisted solely of him and the man he faced. Christina felt chilled and vaguely hurt. He'd never even glanced at their seats to see if she and Albert had arrived safely.

Telling herself that she was being unreasonable, that Jace was a professional, so of course he'd concentrate on the game, she settled back to watch him pitch. She winced the first time he threw the ball and jarred his leg when he landed, but she could see no sign of pain in his face. It must really be healed, she thought in relief.

"He's doing great!" Albert enthused two innings later. "That's the fifth batter he's struck out. I wonder if they'll yank him for a pinch hitter?"

"Yank?" Christina blinked.

"Take him out," Albert explained. "This is the National league, remember. Pitchers bat for themselves."

"Not very well from what I remember," she said dryly.

"McCormick's a pretty good hitting pitcher." The man in the seat beside her joined the conversation. "You two Lancers' fans?"

"We sure are! Jace is my cousin," Albert related with pride.

"Well, imagine that." The man looked impressed enough even for Albert. "Do you suppose you could get him to autograph my program?"

"Well..." Albert looked doubtful.

"Put your name and address on it, and we'll mail it to you after he signs it," Christina suggested.

"Thanks a lot, lady." The man grinned in delight.

"Lookee, Christina," Albert claimed her attention. "Jace's going to bat for himself."

"A moment of high drama, I take it." She smiled at the little boy, but her humor was short-lived as the opposing pitcher threw the ball inches from Jace's head.

"You gutless yellow belly," Albert screamed in rage. "You're trying to hit him 'cause he's better than you. He doesn't have to throw beanballs."

Jace ignored Albert, but to Christina's surprise, a dark tide stained the opposing pitcher's cheeks. Not that it improved his aim. He reared back and flung the ball, again missing Jace's head by inches.

Christina gasped in horror, and the man beside her said, "Don't worry. The brushback pitch's just a part of the game."

"Just a part of the game!" she repeated incredulously. "Getting smacked in the head by a ninety-mile-an-hour fastball is just a part of the game?"

The man shrugged. "Why do you think they pay McCormick all that money? Getting hit's an occupational hazard."

Christina bit back an urge to tell the cretin beside her exactly what she thought of him, his ancestry, his attitude and what he could do with his desire for Jace's autograph. She held her breath as the pitcher wound up again, this time throwing it behind Jace's back. The ball rolled to the backstop with the catcher scrambling after it.

"That so-called pitcher is a menace," she muttered.

"Naw, he's just erratic." The man seemed unaware of her anger. "Course now, he's never going to be another Jace McCormick. You only get a pitcher like him every once in a blue moon, but—" He broke off as the pitcher threw the ball again and it sailed over Jace's head.

"Ah," Albert muttered in satisfaction as Jace trotted down to first base and the umpire headed toward the Reds' dugout.

"What happened besides Jace's walk?" Christina watched as the Reds' manager gestured angrily at the umpire.

"I bet the umpire warned the bench," Albert said. "If the pitcher throws at anyone again, he'll be ejected."

"Talk about locking the barn after the horse has been stolen," Christina grumbled.

"Damn bunch of wimps," the man complained. "In the old days, no one minded a bit of blood."

"The way things are going I'm feeling older by the minute," Christina said tartly.

"Another seven innings and it's over, Christina," Albert comforted her, "and then we can meet Jace for dinner."

"Say—" the man gave him a considering look "—I could come along with you and get Jace's autograph myself."

"No." Christina took a great deal of satisfaction in denying his request. It was the last satisfaction she got until the Lancers' manager removed Jace from the game after the sixth inning. From then on it was simply a matter of waiting until the interminable game was over and they could meet Jace.

Eight

There's Jace! Just coming in the door behind that guy with the suitcases.'' Albert bounced out of his chair and raced across the hotel lobby toward him.

Christina got to her feet a little more slowly, her eyes narrowing as she warily studied Jace. To her relief, the single-minded concentration that had marked his features during the game was gone, replaced by his normal look of alert, amused intelligence.

But her relief was short-lived as she watched Albert rudely shoved aside by someone in the crowd that had seemed to magically form around Jace. Hastily she started to rescue him, but her intervention proved unnecessary. Jace saw the boy and, reaching out, drew him up against his side.

Christina smiled as Albert preened himself at the obvious envy of the other children. She moved to the perimeter of the crowd and watched while Jace signed autographs. He was very good with the kids, she noted as he patiently listened to them tell him about their Little League experiences. And he was very good with their mothers, too, she thought on a flash of hot feeling as Jace signed a woman's program and handed it back to her with a warm grin. Christina forced herself to probe her unusual reaction and was appalled to realize that what she was feeling was nothing more than plain old-fashioned jealousy. It was a sobering thought.

She'd never been jealous over a man in her life, and yet here she was contemplating forcibly yanking away the overblown brunette who was practically drooling all over Jace. Jace was hers, Christina wanted to tell the woman in no uncertain terms. And that impulse confused her further. She'd always believed that people didn't belong to other people. They belonged to themselves. That relationships needed lots of space to thrive and yet now, inexplicably, she wanted to publicly claim Jace. Making love to Jace had temporarily thrown her off balance, she said to herself, excusing her aberration. In a few days she'd be back to her normal, rational self.

As if to give lie to her conclusion, Jace looked up, caught sight of her and gave her a slow sensual smile that ignited a blaze of desire deep within her.

The brunette turned to see who Jace was smiling at, gave Christina a disgruntled look and moved away, clutching her youngster in one hand and Jace's autograph in the other.

"Is it always like this?" Christina asked Jace when he and Albert finally joined her.

"Not in visiting cities. This is probably just because it's my first start since my injury," he said. "Come on, let's go in to dinner before we get cornered again."

"Gosh, Jace, everybody knows you," Albert said admiringly.

"Some better than others." Jace gave Christina a warm look over the little boy's head.

Christina licked her suddenly dry lips and stared back, unable to control the answering rush of desire that sent a warm flush along her cheekbones.

"Good evening, Jace." The hostess at the hotel's restaurant gave him a beaming smile. "Congratulations on your win today."

"Thank you." Jace shepherded Albert and the curious Christina to their table. Did Jace know every woman in this town, she wondered. Or only the attractive ones?

"Who was that?" Albert, apparently wondering, too, asked the question Christina had too much pride to ask.

"Who?" Jace looked around the crowded restaurant in confusion.

"That lady that showed us to our seats."

Jace shrugged. "I haven't the vaguest idea."

"But she called you Jace," Albert insisted.

"Sports figures tend to get called by their first name for some reason. Now, enough of the fickle public. Tell me how you two have been getting along while I've been gone?"

"We missed you," Albert said plaintively.

"Did you?" Jace gave Christina a penetrating glance and she hung on to her composure with an effort. It would never do to give him the idea that she felt she had some kind of claim on him simply because they'd made love. From the look of things this afternoon, he already had far too many people trying to make claims on him.

"Yeah. It's lonesome with just Christina and me," Albert continued. "But lots of people came by, and the sheriff let me turn on his siren and flash his lights."

"Did Christina get to turn anything on?" His sensual grin short-circuited her breathing.

"I'd like to turn a few things off," she said.

"Aw, the siren wasn't that loud," Albert muttered, oblivious to the undercurrents.

"Why was the sheriff there in the first place?" Jace queried.

"He stopped by to let me know they'd been keeping an eye on the house while we were there by ourselves," Christina explained.

"Good." Jace nodded in satisfaction. "Now, then, what would you two like to eat? I'm starved. I was too nervous to eat before the game."

But despite Jace's hunger, he wasn't given much opportunity to enjoy his meal. They were constantly interrupted by other diners who stopped by their table to either congratulate him on his win or to ask him for his autograph.

Christina fumed inwardly at their lack of consideration, but two things stopped her from giving way to her annoyance. First of all, it was Jace they were bothering and he gave every appearance of being quite delighted to talk to them, and, more importantly, the people were almost without exception family groups with children.

"Honestly," she complained during a lull in the stream of fans, "I haven't had so many interruptions at dinner since the night I baby-sat Albert when he was two months old and had the colic."

"Sorry," Jace apologized. "We should have eaten in my room."

"You shouldn't have to hide out in your room just because other people have no consideration," Christina said emphatically. "They shouldn't—" She broke off as an elderly lady came up and asked for an autograph for her grandson who, she assured Jace, was going to be so thrilled.

It was nice someone was going to be thrilled, Christina thought grimly, staring down at her rapidly cooling dinner. Because she sure wasn't. Jace couldn't even appear in public without being accosted by absolute strangers who seemed to feel that simply because they were fans they had the right to demand his time and attention.

She didn't understand how he could tolerate such an appalling lack of privacy. She'd only been subjected to it for a few hours and already her nerves were jangled, her stomach hurt and a dull throbbing was starting behind her eyes.

Jace, after a searching look at her tense features, threw his napkin down beside his plate and said, "Come on. Let's go up to my room and relax."

"I'd love to." Christina gave him a relieved smile. She'd never ask him to hide out from his fans, but if he offered she was certainly willing to accept.

"Quick, a fan is bearing down on us at eight o'clock," Christina whispered.

"Do you know that the word *fan* is derived from fanatic?" Jace pretended not to see the man as he put a hand on the small of her back to guide her out of the restaurant.

Christina barely suppressed the shiver that coursed over her skin at his light touch. This was awful, she thought in dismay. Despite the fact that she was tense and upset, the slightest contact with Jace still had the power to throw her emotions into a state of absolute confusion.

"Just a second." Jace suddenly stopped as they reached the bank of elevators. "I forgot to check the desk for messages. Wait here. I won't be long." He walked back to the front desk, and Albert wandered over to the fountain in the middle of the lobby.

As Jace spoke to the clerk, Christina watched, dreamily studying the way the sparkling lights from the overhead chandelier created reddish highlights in his dark hair. She swallowed longingly. He really was an incredibly attractive man.

It quickly became obvious that her opinion was shared by at least one other person in the lobby. As Christina watched, a girl who couldn't have been more than eighteen sauntered over to him, her long shapely legs displayed to advantage in skintight jeans. A deeply cut, closely fitted, ribbed top left little of her overabundant charms to the imagination.

"Hello, there." The girl leaned toward Jace, every line in her body a sensual enticement.

Christina watched in disbelief, having no idea how to deal with the situation. She'd never been out with a man before who'd been propositioned while within her hearing range. It was like something out of a badly written soap opera entitled *Man Pursued by Sex-Hungry Hordes of Women*. She swallowed against an almost hysterical urge to laugh. It really wasn't funny. It was frightening. She felt as if she were being threatened by a mob of people all wearing smiles.

"I've been dying to meet you." The girl's husky whisper was a masterpiece of seductive promise.

"And now you have." Jace gave the girl a dismissive nod and, accepting several sheets of paper from the clerk, started toward Christina.

"Sorry about that." Jace took her arm and with a call to Albert hurried them into the elevator.

"That kid practically propositioned you," Christina said tightly.

"That kid probably knows more about se—life," he substituted after a quick look at Albert, "than you and I combined."

"Everybody knows about sexual urges," Albert said unconcernedly.

"It certainly seems so," Christina said tightly, wishing she'd never come today. She'd seen Jace all right, but she'd also seen what kind of life he normally led. He lived in the proverbial fishbowl. A fishbowl full of temptation. Would he have accepted the girl's invitation if she hadn't been there? The question nagged at her. She knew Jace was a man of strong passion. Knew it from personal experience. But personal experience also told her that he was fastidious, as well as intelligent, she reminded herself. Much too intelligent to engage in a series of one-night stands with strangers.

"I'm just down the hall to your right." Jace held the elevator doors for them.

"Can I order something from room service?" Albert asked.

"You can't possibly be hungry," Christina heard herself say, vaguely surprised that she could respond so naturally while her emotions were churning in such violent circles.

Jace unlocked the door to his room and, sticking his head in, called, "Dave, are you here?"

"Not for long." A tall man emerged from the bathroom. "Some of us are going out for the evening. Hi." He smiled at Christina. "I'm Dave Wilson."

"Christina Hollowell and this is Albert." She forced a smile, even though her face felt as if it might break from the effort.

Dave glanced from her rigid features to Jace's and then as if in response to an unspoken plea said, "Some of the guys from the team are going to Kings Island, Albert. You want to come with us?"

"Kings Island?" Albert's eyes lit up with pleasure at the thought of meeting some more of Jace's teammates.

"It's an amusement park. A big one."

"Can I go, Christina? Can I, huh, please?" Albert begged.

Christina looked at Jace. She didn't know who Dave was or where this park was or when they'd be back. And what was worse, she was finding it hard to care. All she wanted to do was to run. Run back to Boston where she'd be safe.

"Great idea, Dave." Jace gave him a grateful smile.

"We'll be back about eleven. Come on, Albert. If we don't hurry, they'll leave without us." Dave hustled the boy out the door.

Jace closed and latched it behind them and then turned to Christina and said, "What's wrong? You've been acting strangely all evening."

"Me!" The word exploded from her. "That's great coming from you."

He blinked at the vehemence of her reaction. "What's wrong with me?"

"What isn't wrong with you," she shot back. "First, we arrive at the ballpark and it's like you're some stranger on the mound. Even your facial expression was different."

"I was concentrating," he said patiently. "There's a whole lot more to pitching than simply throwing the ball as hard as you can."

"And you never even waved or spoke to us on your way into the dugout." To her dismay, her hurt at being ignored popped out.

"Listen, Christina, if I'd given even the slightest inkling that I knew you, there'd have been at least one reporter hounding you, asking you the most impertinent questions. I didn't want to subject you to that." His large hand closed over her chilled fingers, sending eddies of warmth through them.

"But it's more than my not saying hello, isn't it, Christina?" His fingers began an insidious stroking over the back of her hand. "You've been getting more and more tense all through dinner. What's wrong?"

"Everything." She sighed despairingly. "I thought the way your neighbors back at the farm treated you was bad enough, but it's negligible compared to what I saw today. I don't see how you live like this. You can't even eat in peace, and that apprentice Lolita..." She stopped, afraid of revealing her blazing jealousy. "I feel like I don't know you. As if you've turned into somebody else."

"Close your eyes, Christina," Jace ordered.

"But what—"

"Close them," he repeated softly, and she did.

At first, all she felt was the soft warmth of his breath on her face. Then he leaned closer and the heat from his body encircled her, carrying with it the faintly elusive scent of his cologne.

Christina held her body rigid against the appeal of his nearness. She didn't need this, her mind informed her in silent warning. Not now. Not when she was already so confused and upset. She just couldn't deal with the emotional turmoil his touch caused.

"Jace." She began to open her eyes, but he forestalled the motion by kissing her fluttering eyelids.

"Don't look at me with your eyes, Christina," he murmured. "Look with your heart."

Christina felt the rough texture of his fingertips as he traced over her left eyebrow and then moved downward to explore the indentations of her ear.

"I..." The words came out on a long, shuddering sigh.

"No. No words. Don't think. Just feel." He brushed her loose curls back from her forehead and, leaning closer, traced the faint blue veins beneath the pale skin on her temple with the tip of his tongue.

A spasm went through her as the remembered heat began to build.

"Look with your heart," he repeated, a thin thread of some jagged emotion she couldn't quite identify coloring his voice.

Christina reached for him. Her hand cupped his chin and she felt the strength in it. The strength in him. Her fingers moved upward, over his mouth and her heart lurched into a slow, heavy rhythm as her own lips began to tingle at the remembered feel of his.

Her hands slipped down to skim over his broad shoulders and then down his chest, feeling the hard, heavy beat of his heart.

His skin was hot and damp with need. Need for her. The knowledge bubbled through her like the most powerful aphrodisiac and she began to tremble.

Feeling her response, Jace swept her up in his arms and gently set her down on the bed. His fingers unbuttoned the soft scarlet silk of her blouse and pushed it apart. Because of the heat, she'd dispensed with a bra, and Jace's indrawn breath was a clear indication that he approved.

"You're exquisite, Christina." His fingertips grazed the tips of her breasts, turning them into tight, swollen buds, aching for the touch of his mouth.

He hastily shrugged out of his clothes, carelessly flinging them onto the floor before he fell down on the bed beside her.

His hand cupped her breast, and he kneaded the soft flesh for a moment before taking it in his mouth and suckling. Christina inhaled sharply as desire began to fog her mind.

"I can't think," she muttered.

"Don't think, feel!" The desperation in his voice reached her as nothing else could have. She didn't understand it. All she knew was that it was intolerable that Jace should feel it. Instinctively, she reached for him, her fingers clutching his shoulders. The heat of his skin startled her and she pulled him closer, offering him the comfort of her body.

"Oh, yes, my love." His husky endearment rewarded her. With a supple movement, he covered her body with his, sending an arrow of pleasure shooting through her. For a brief second, her heart stopped beating and then plunged into a thunderous rhythm that made her body throb with longing.

Her long legs moved restlessly, and Jace trapped them between his thighs. Raising himself on his elbows, he rubbed his chest across her breasts, his crisp body hair rasped against her already sensitized nipples, sending a piercing hunger through her.

The hard ridge of his manhood pressed against her abdomen like a branding iron.

He stared down into her flushed features and said, "Those people aren't important. This is what's important. What we have."

But what did they have? Christina almost cried her frustration aloud. What did Jace think they had that he was so desperate to protect? Just sex? Christina stared up at him, trying to read the answer in his taut features. It was impossible.

With a soft sigh of surrender, she wrapped her arms around his neck and pulled him down to her. He was partly right. Those people didn't matter now. Right now nothing mattered but how they could make each other feel.

Deliberately banishing her fears, she arched upwards, seeking the ultimate embrace. Seeking to become part of him.

He lifted himself off her, then pulled her skirt up to her waist and yanked her bikini panties down over her legs with unsteady fingers.

His mouth closed over hers and his tongue pushed inside, its slow, hot pressure a torment to her beleaguered senses. A torment that intensified unbearably as he stroked tantalizingly over the very heart of her femininity with his finger. He greedily swallowed her aching whimper of longing as one of his fingers entered her.

Christina went rigid in an agony of anticipation and then twisted frantically as he began to slowly caress the very center of her desire. Feverishly she tried to pull him down to her, but he held back, trapping her in the tormentingly slow rhythm.

She tore her mouth away from his and cried, "Please, Jace, I can't wait any longer."

In answer to her plea, he lowered his body slightly. She could feel the heat of him pressing against her, and she raised her hips, desperate to feel him within her. Boldly he surged forward, fusing their bodies together.

Christina sighed, as for a brief moment his act of possession made her feel complete. Then he moved slightly and her sense of contentment was swallowed up in a desire so intense that her body started to quiver. She wrapped her legs around his hips, straining upward to meet each of his deep thrusts, the pleasure so intense she could hardly bear it. She felt as if she were coming apart inside. Seconds later, her high keening cry of intense pleasure drove him to faster and deeper thrusts, until suddenly he went rigid with his own satifaction, and then he collapsed on her.

Christina smiled euphorically as she ran her fingers across the sweat-dampened slickness of his back and then traced up his spine, hesitating when he twitched.

"Don't." Jace rolled onto his side and drew her into his arms, binding her tightly to him. "I'm ticklish."

"You are?" Her eyes began to gleam with mischief.

"I'm also much bigger than you are," he warned.

"Big deal. What are you going to do, wrestle me?" she scoffed, secure in the knowledge that Jace would never hurt her. Not intentionally.

"No, what I'll do is kiss you senseless and then make love to you till you can't think straight, let alone torture me."

"Oh?" She forced herself to meet his eyes. She had no reason to be shy of Jace, she assured herself. Not when he made her feel like a voluptuous, desirable woman. And that was how she intended to act, she decided on a burst of determination.

"Christina." He cupped her face between his hands and stared into her deep blue eyes. "Did you understand the point I was trying to make? That's I'm still the person I was on the farm. It's the people around us who are different, and they don't count. Christina?" He gently shook her when she didn't respond, vaguely annoyed that he'd forced her to face the problem again.

"Well, you're right about part of it," she said. "You're the same person you were on the farm. I was simply seeing another facet of your personality out on the mound today, that of an intense competitor. If I'd thought about it, I'd have realized that anyone who approached plant breeding with the fervor that you do would apply that same intensity to other areas of his life, as well." Such as his lovemaking. A soft, dreamy smile curved her lips.

"But?" He probed at her abstracted expression.

"But the people around you do make a difference. My God, Jace, how do you live like this? With everybody seeming to think they have a right to make demands on your time. Or your body!" Her voice hardened at the thought of the girl in the lobby.

"My time I give freely to my fans, but no one makes demands on my body," he replied patiently. "I'm a fully grown, adult male. I can say no quite effectively."

"And do you when you're by yourself?" The question popped out even though she knew she had no right to ask it.

"Always," he said emphatically. "I haven't had the slightest desire to collect notches on my bedpost since I was eighteen. Casual sex is strictly for the birds. Besides, in this day and age it can be downright dangerous.''

''I see.'' Christina carefully studied his earnest features, trying to decipher the exact meaning behind his words. If he didn't consider their lovemaking casual sex, then what did he consider it? Was he as drawn to her as she was to him? There was no way to know without asking, and she had no intention of laying herself open to the pain that might be caused by the stark truth.

''But you still aren't convinced, are you?'' His voice hardened as he got to his feet and began to shrug into his clothes.

Christina felt a chill feather over her skin, but she still persisted.

''I believe you about the women who fling themselves at you, Jace, but I can't quite be so accepting of all those people who kept pestering you at dinner.''

''They're basically nice people who don't stop to think. And I'm willing to admit that there are times when they're a pain in the neck. But you have to remember—it's the fans who pay my salary. They have a right to be treated with respect even if they're behaving thoughtlessly.''

''Perhaps.'' She got up, suddenly embarrassed to be naked while he was dressed. ''Would it be all right if I used your shower?''

''Certainly.'' He picked up the phone, his mind clearly elsewhere. A tiny pang of hurt went through her at the ease with which he seemed to dismiss her from his thoughts, but she refused to allow it to fester. Time was on her side. Their mutual concern over Albert would keep them in close contact for the foreseeable future. She could afford to slowly nurture Jace's growing feelings for her without having to risk forcing the issue.

The shower helped to dispel her lingering unease, and she returned to the bedroom, feeling much more alert and capable of dealing with the whole situation. One thing of which she was absolutely certain was that Jace was worth fighting for.

"I'm not asking you, Larry. I'm telling you." Jace's biting tones riveted her attention. His face was set in harsh lines and his body was stiff with tension.

Christina frowned. Who was Larry and what did he want?

"I don't give a damn," Jace snapped. "That's the way it's going to be." He listened to the voice at the other end for a few minutes and then said, "You have my word. I'll be there. Good luck."

Jace hung up and stared blindly out the window, his fingers absently rubbing over his jawline.

Christina watched the hypnotic movement for a few seconds and then asked, "Who's Larry?"

"What?" Jace blinked as if surprised to see her.

"Who's Larry?" she repeated.

"The Lancers' general manager," Jace replied.

"You certainly didn't sound very happy with him?" she probed.

"No one's happy with Larry. He's a gold-plated, first-class jerk."

Christina chuckled. "He must have some good points?"

"Those were his good points." Jace grinned. "Come on. We've got the whole evening before us. Let's sneak out of the hotel and do some sight-seeing ourselves."

"I'd love to." A flare of excitement kindled through her at the thought of spending an evening alone with him.

"Oh, dear." Her pleasure faded somewhat as she suddenly realized something.

"What's the matter?" Jace asked.

"If Albert doesn't get back until eleven, I'll be driving over strange roads in the middle of the night. But I don't suppose it matters." She tried to shrug off her concern.

"Not at all—" Jace unlocked the door and swung it open "—since I'll be coming back with you."

"What?" Christina stared apprehensively at his knee, suddenly fearful that he'd somehow managed to reinjure himself. "What did you do to yourself?"

His eyes swung back to the now-rumpled bed. "Pleasured myself beyond my wildest dreams." He gave her a smile that made her want to forget sight-seeing and investigate the wonders a little closer to home. She stifled the urge in favor of finding out what was wrong.

"Quit beating around the bush and get to the facts. Did you reinjure your knee?"

"No," he answered succinctly. "Nor any other part of my anatomy, although it felt like your nails left some interesting marks on my back."

"Sorry," she muttered.

"Sweetheart, you can leave marks all over my body any time you like." He gave her a look that could only be described as a leer.

"Well, you can't avoid the issue by embarrassing me," she insisted.

"There's nothing wrong with my knee," he said, "but there's also no real reason for me to travel with the team. I'm not scheduled to pitch again until Friday. I can easily fly up to Chicago to join the Lancers on Thursday night."

"Great." The very real pleasure she felt at the thought of Jace being home for four days added a silvery brilliance to her deep blue eyes. She craved contact with him. Craved it with an increasing urgency that worried her. "It was nice of the Lancers to let you rest at home till your next start."

"Uh-huh." Jace turned back to lock the door behind them so that she missed the rueful look that crossed his face at her words.

Nine

———

Jace pulled the car up in front of the house and, aiming the device on his dashboard at it, turned on his inside lights.

"You unlock the door," Jace whispered to Christina, "and I'll carry Albert in."

"I'll walk. I'm awake," Albert mumbled from the back seat.

"Well, you shouldn't be. It's—" Christina checked the digital clock on the dashboard "—nearly three o'clock in the morning."

"I don't care. I had a fantastic time at Kings Island. I rode everything. When can we go again?"

"When you can find another dupe to take you," she said. "I don't ride anything. I've got better sense."

Jace chuckled. "What you've got is no sense of adventure. It's 'cause she's a girl," he whispered in an audible aside to Albert.

"That's right," she agreed smugly. "Women have better sense than to risk life and limb for a few thrills. Now, if you two are through with your sexist discussion, let's go inside."

"It really was a neat park." Albert trailed along behind her, his steps none too steady. "And the guys were really great, too. Can we come to see you pitch another game, Jace?"

"The season's almost over. There won't be that many more games." Jace unlocked the front door and swung it open, barely missing Jasper's twitching nose.

"What's the matter, animal, did you miss us?" Jace hefted the beast into his arms and absently scratched behind his ears.

"But you'll pitch lots more," Albert persisted, "and I—"

"Should be in school, not flitting across the countryside, following a baseball team," Jace cut him off. "Now go on to bed, it's very late."

"I hate school! It spoils everything." Albert stomped down the hall, and Christina frowned as she watched him go.

Albert's request to watch Jace pitch again hadn't been that unreasonable. It would have been an easy matter for her and Albert to fly up to Chicago on Friday. He would have only had to miss one day of school, which was insignificant for a student of Albert's caliber. So why didn't Jace want them to come? Especially since their going to Cincinatti had been his idea in the first place. His sudden about-face made her very uneasy. It was as if he'd suddenly thought better of involving her in all aspects of his life.

"Would you like a nightcap, Christina?" Jace set the rabbit down and picked up the mail that had accumulated during his absence.

"No, thanks." Christina forgot her doubts about his motives in the face of a much more immediate problem. Did Jace expect her to share his bed, or was his refusal to invite them to Chicago a sign that he was trying to draw back from their relationship?

She rubbed her throbbing forehead in frustration. Three in the morning was not the best time to be trying to figure out the intricacies of their relationship.

She stole a quick glance at Jace, but he was reading a letter, seemingly engrossed in it. Although, perhaps, his very absorption in the mail was her answer. Her stomach twitched nervously. Surely, if he expected her to share his bed, he'd be a little more amorous. Unless . . . She frowned as she suddenly remembered Albert. Unless, Jace was afraid Albert would react negatively to their sharing a bedroom even though he seemed to find nothing out of the ordinary about their kissing each other?

She sighed in desperation. It was possible. Anything was possible, and at this time of night, anything seemed probable.

"Tired?" Jace eyed her sharply.

"I was just trying to summon the energy to go to bed. If you'll excuse me, I'll be off."

"Good night." He gave her a smile. "I'll turn in as soon as I finish checking the mail."

Yes, but whose bed was he going to turn in to, Christina wondered as she headed toward her own room. She might have come a long way in thinking of herself as a desirable, sexy woman, but not so far that she could jump into his bed without a specific invitation.

Christina rushed through her normal bedtime routine with the vague thought of already being in bed if he did come. But to her intense disappointment, when she finally heard his footsteps, they continued on past her room and down the hall to his own.

Christina expelled her pent up breath on an accepting sigh. That was that. Their relationship did not include an open acknowledgment of the fact that they were lovers. But maybe it was for the best, she tried to tell herself. Albert might react negatively, and Albert had to be their first concern.

It took her almost an hour to fall asleep, and then it was a restless sleep, filled with vague longings that seemed forever out of reach. Finally her troubling dreams slipped into a full-blown nightmare of horrific proportions. Struggling out of it, she forced open eyelids that felt glued together, to find herself staring into a pair of beady black eyes.

"You idiot animal!" Christina pushed Jasper off her chest. No wonder she was having nightmares, with that overfed lump sitting on her. She was lucky she hadn't suffocated.

"How did you get in here?" She glanced at the door to find it ajar. Had Jace changed his mind and come to join her only to find her asleep?

"Oh, good, you're awake, Christina." Albert's beaming little face appeared around the door. "I checked earlier, but you were snoring."

"I don't snore," she said reprovingly.

"Okay, you were snuffling," Albert agreed happily. "Jace said to tell you breakfast is almost ready. We're making pancakes. You can have my first batch," he said and then left.

Yeah, and I'll bet I also get stuck with the mess to clean up, she thought grumpily as she dropped Jasper onto the floor. She wondered why Jace had sent Albert to wake her up instead of coming to do it himself. Was he trying to drive home the fact that their involvement was to remain secret?

Or was he simply flipping pancakes and couldn't leave them, she mocked her fears. The answer could quite possibly be as innocuous as that and they best way to find out would be to join them for breakfast.

She hurriedly dressed and arrived in the kitchen just in time to see Albert trying to catch a flying pancake in a frying pan. He missed, and the half-cooked pancake landed on the counter with a splat.

"Definitely a mess," she muttered. Pouring herself a cup of black coffee, she took a fortifying gulp and asked, "Why was that pancake airborne?"

"I'm practicing." Albert looked up from the task of pouring more batter into the sizzling pan. "Did you know Jace can flip pancakes real high?" he asked enthusiastically.

"So can you." She stole a look at Jace and he gave her a smug grin. The very normalcy of his expression soothed her jumpy nerves, even if it didn't answer any of her questions.

"Yeah, but Jace's land in the pan," Albert said mournfully.

"He's had more practice than you," Christina comforted him. "After all, he's four times your age."

"Four times!" Albert's eyes widened, and he stared at Jace rather as if he expected him to fall apart before his eyes.

"Do you two mind." Jace finished cleaning up the squashed pancake. "I'm sensitive about my age. Thirty-six in the baseball world is almost over the hill."

"Oh, I think you've got a few good years left." Christina's eyes involuntarily strayed down his body.

Jace's knowing chuckle brought her to her senses, and she tore her gaze away in time to see another of Albert's pancakes come to grief on the floor.

"You know, Albert, that looks like a skill best perfected outdoors. Like when you're camping," she suggested.

"But you hate camping," Albert reminded her. "You'd never come with Mom and Dad and me."

"I'll bet Jace likes camping." Christina gave the wary-looking Jace a malicious grin. "Big, strong athletic types are very into outdoor sports."

"Great." Albert gave Jace a beaming smile. "I love living in a tent and sleeping on the ground. When can we go?"

"We'll all go," he said with a look at Christina that promised retribution. "Just as soon as the baseball season's over. The possibility of a killing frost will add a certain piquancy to the situation, don't you agree, Christina?"

"The whole idea's killing," she grumbled. "Mankind spends millions of years evolving into civilized beings with gas and electricity and Hyatt Regencies and what do you want to do? Sit on the cold hard ground and stare at a smoldering fire. Now, do you call that logical?"

"No, I call it fun." Albert shoved a plate of misshapen pancakes in front of her.

"To each his own." She reached for the syrup, liberally dousing the pancakes before taking a bite, trying to ignore the texture of the uncooked middle.

"Fantastic," she told the anxiously waiting Albert.

"Do you really think so?" Albert asked uncertainly.

"Absolutely." She took a second bite. "You're a great cook. In fact, to show my appreciation, I'll even clean up the kitchen."

"Gee, thanks, Christina," Albert accepted. "Ryan and I are going caving after breakfast. Ryan says he knows where lots are."

"I don't know about Ryan, but you are going to spend the rest of your life in your room if you so much as set one foot in a cave without an adult being there."

"Aw, Christina, caving's fun," Albert wailed.

"It's also dangerous and incredibly stupid to go into a strange cave without the proper equipment," Jace said flatly. "You and Ryan can locate all the caves you want, but if you go down one..." His threat was all the more potent for being unstated.

"That's not fair!" Albert yelled. "Ryan can go into them. He'll think I'm a sissy."

"If you're that keen to go caving, we could visit Mammoth Cave in Kentucky after the season," Jace offered.

"Ryan, too?" Albert bargained.

"Ryan, too," Jace agreed, and Albert, his good humor restored, tore out the door to share the news with his friend.

Christina pushed her plate away and reached for her coffee.

"What's the matter?" Jace noticed her frown.

"I don't like the way you keep promising treats after the season's over," she said. "You know perfectly well Albert isn't going to be here. He'll be home with me in Boston."

"Do you still think I'd be such a terrible guardian?" Jace looked strangely hurt.

Christina froze for a second, remembering her earlier fears that he'd made love to her in order to get her to agree to give up Albert. No, she immediately dismissed the thought. Jace wouldn't do that. He had too much basic integrity. An integrity that somehow had survived the adulation of his fans.

"No," she finally said. "I was wrong in my initial judgment of you. Actually, in the abstract, you'd make a great guardian for Albert. Probably better than I would—" she forced herself to admit the painful truth "—because you're a man and he'll need a man more as he grows older. But the fact remains that as many admirable qualities as you have, you simply aren't around for long periods of time."

"I know and I'm working on it," he said.

"I—"

"Christina! Jace! Ryan's Uncle Joe broke his leg!" Albert rushed back into the kitchen to deliver the news in ecstatic tones.

"Far be it from me to dampen your enthusiasm, my boy," Christina said, "but in this culture it's usually considered normal to at least pretend a feeling of regret when someone hurts himself."

"But don't you see, he's in the hospital," Ryan offered from behind Albert.

Christina shook her head. "Actually, no, I don't see at all. What is it with you two apprentice ghouls?"

"If'n Uncle Joe's in the hospital, then my Aunt Sue can't leave him," Ryan began.

Jace nodded. "Sounds reasonable so far."

"And if'n Uncle Joe's in the hospital and Aunt Sue can't leave him, then they can't use their tickets to the Colts game this afternoon."

Christina blinked. "Colts?"

"Indianapolis Colts, they're a football team in the AFC East," Albert said impatiently at her blank look.

"Ah, the light dawns." Christina nodded sagely. "You two are to be the recipients of Uncle Joe's largess."

"Naw, we get to use his tickets," Ryan said.

"Quite." Jace shot Christina a laughing glance.

"Yeah, my dad, he said me and Albert might as well come along."

"Please, can I go, huh, please?" Albert begged.

"If you promise to wear a seat belt on the trip," Christina said.

"No problem about that, ma'am," Ryan offered. "Nobody rides in my dad's car unless'n they wear a seat belt. My dad, he says his mom didn't raise no idiot."

"Your dad's right." Christina nodded emphatically.

"Can I have some money to buy a souvenir with, Christina," Albert asked.

Jace shot a quick glance at the suddenly solemn-looking Ryan and said, "Tell you what, boys, since Mr. Evans is supplying the tickets, it only seems fair that I should supply the food and souvenirs." He took out his wallet and gave each boy a twenty-dollar bill.

"Gee, thanks, Jace. I'll be right back after the game. If you watch it on TV, maybe you'll see me in the stands." Albert grabbed the stunned-looking Ryan and practically dragged him out of the kitchen.

"Now, why would any sane person spend a perfectly gorgeous Sunday afternoon plunked down in front of a TV set?" she yelled after him.

"I'll say, especially when there are so many more interesting things to be doing on a quiet Sunday afternoon," Jace's husky voice shortened her breathing.

"Oh?" Christina's glance collided with the smoldering look in his eyes and then fell to the tabletop as she tried to think. It was impossible. She was too busy feeling. Feeling the sensitive skin of her abdomen flutter at the memory of his weight against it, feeling the ache building in her breasts at the memory of his hot mouth on them, feeling the tingling of her lips at the memory of his hard kisses. This was awful, she thought in horror. She was becoming so sensitized to his touch that merely the memory of his lovemaking was sufficient to reduce her to a mindless mass of desire.

"Yes, 'oh.'" Jace leaned over and dropped a quick kiss on the end of her nose, and Christina jumped as a shower of sparks cascaded over her skin.

"Don't fix lunch, we'll send out for pizza afterward." Jace's eyes gleamed with promise. "In the meantime, if you want me, I'll be out in the garden."

Oh, she wanted him all right. Christina watched him go, filled with a confusing mixture of emotions, but overriding them all was excited anticipation. Apparently her assumption last night had been the right one. Jace didn't want Albert to know they were lovers, but even though she didn't fully agree with his decision, she could understand why he felt that way and, for the moment, she was willing to go along with it.

She finished her coffee and got to her feet, intending to take care of a few odds and ends while Jace was outside. On her way to make the beds, she found Jace's suitcase, which he'd brought back from Cincinatti, and decided to wash a few loads of laundry. Opening the suitcase, she set it on the dryer and began to sort through the jumble of garments. She tossed the whites into the washer and the coloreds into the laundry basket. Then she set the leather toiletry bag and his baseball glove on the shelf above the washer. She started the cycle and, leaving the washing machine lid up to remind her to add bleach once the tub was full of water, she went back to the kitchen to load the dishwasher.

She was halfway through when Jace pushed open the kitchen door and demanded, "What did you do with my pesticide? The squash need another application."

"Who, me?" She gave him a look of wide-eyed innocence. "I don't use poisons. What would I do with it?"

"Dammit, Christina, what did you do with it? I need it."

"You don't need poison. You need to get rid of the squash borers," she countered. "I'd be glad to lend a hand as soon as I finish in here."

"If you don't tell me where it is, I'll go into town and buy some more," he threatened.

"Not today you won't. The farm store's closed on Sunday. You'd do better to take me up on my offer."

"I'd like to take you to a psychiatrist for treatment for your closed mind," he said in frustration.

"My closed mind! Your mind is set in concrete. Do you want my help or not?"

"Help like yours could set the entire field of agriculture back a hundred years. And put some sunscreen on your face before you come out. The sun's hotter than hell." He stomped out of the room.

Christina watched him go, wondering just how annoyed he really was. Maybe she should give him back his pesticide. After all, he wasn't doing anything more than ninety-nine percent of the farmers in America were doing. Why was it so important to her that she convert him to chemical-free gardening? She tried to analyze her motives. Because Albert looked up to him as an authority figure, she finally decided, refusing to probe any deeper.

She'd almost finished cleaning the kitchen before she remembered the laundry. When she saw the lid still up on the washing machine, she grimaced in annoyance. She'd forgotten to put in the bleach. She just hoped everything had come out clean.

Christina was busily transferring the wet clothes from the washer to the dryer when, near the bottom, she noticed something dark among the whites. Frowning, she pulled it out. It was a baseball glove. A very wet baseball glove. She stared in puzzlement at it, and then her eyes flew to the shelf above the washer as she suddenly remembered tossing the glove from Jace's suitcase up there. Needless to say it was no longer there. The vibrations from the washer had knocked it off its precarious perch, and, with the washer lid open, it had gone right into the water.

"Oh, dear," she muttered. Jace wasn't going to like this. She eyed the dripping glove in dismay, wondering how much permanent damage the scalding water had done to the leather. But even if she had inadvertently ruined it, he probably had lots of other gloves, she consoled herself. Considering what he was paid, he could afford his own glove factory.

"Christina." Jace stuck his head in the back door. "Quit hiding in the house. You said you'd help and..." He caught sight of the glove in her hand. "Thinking of taking up baseball?" He chuckled as he crossed the room toward her.

"Um, well, actually, it had a slight accident."

"What?"

"The glove. I kind of washed it," she admitted.

"You *what*!" Jace stared at her in disbelief.

"I certainly didn't mean to, but ..."

"Give me that!" Jace grabbed the glove out of her hand, his eyes widening in horror as water oozed out of it.

"Do you know what the hell you've done?" he bellowed.

"I washed your glove and I'm sorry, but it can't be your only one." She held on to her own temper with an effort. She knew he had a right to be annoyed, but surely his reaction was excessive.

"This is the only one that matters!" he yelled. "It's my lucky glove. I always use it down the home stretch of the season. Hell, I carry it myself because I don't trust the equipment manager to do it, and what happens? You *drown* it."

"I didn't realize it was so important," she gritted out. "Perhaps we ought to give it a decent funeral."

"What am I supposed to do now?" he demanded.

"The same thing you always do," she yelled back. "Behave like an overage adolescent."

"I am not an adolescent! I'm a professional who's just had an essential piece of his equipment destroyed by an interfering, meddling—"

"I was trying to help," she defended herself.

"Help what? Help me lose ball games?"

"Why not?" she snapped. "You're losing friends at a fantastic clip."

"Woman, with friends like you, who needs an enemy. You are the most aggravating, opinionated—"

"*I'm* opinionated!" She glared at him. "Oh, that's rich. You with your poisons and your supernatural gloves."

"Oh, hell!" Jace slapped the glove down on the dryer and stormed out of the kitchen, banging the door behind him.

"Oh, hell!" Christina repeated, giving vent to her feelings by slamming the dryer door. "So I'm opinionated, am I?" she demanded of the room at large. "No doubt he prefers women like that oversexed teenager in the hotel who's probably never had a thought that wasn't connected to her libido."

One thing was certain, she decided on a burst of righteous anger. If that's what Jace really thought of her, she had no intention of staying in his house. She stomped down the hall to her bedroom. She and Albert were leaving. Just as soon as he got back from his game. That man wasn't fit to even be around a young impressionable boy, let alone be his guardian. Lucky glove, indeed!

She pulled her suitcase out of the closet and flung it on the bed. Bunch of superstitious mumbo jumbo. Angrily she jerked open a dresser drawer and began to yank her clothes out, haphazardly tossing them into the suitcase.

"What the hell do you think you're doing?" Jace bellowed from the open doorway.

"You're probably smart enough to figure it out yourself. Even without the aid of your lucky glove," she said sharply.

"I liked that glove."

"That much is glaringly obvious, and I did apologize."

"If you hadn't washed it—"

"Never fear, by tomorrow morning my opinionated, aggravating person will no longer be contaminating this hotbed of superstition you call a home."

"I am not superstitious!"

Christina gave him a level stare.

"Well, perhaps a little. About baseball," he conceded. "But that's no reason to carry on like I'm practicing voodoo."

"Maybe irrational behavior is contagious," she sniped.

"I am not irrational and you aren't going anywhere."

"Oh, and how do you intend to stop me? By locking me in a closet?"

"Of all the pigheaded..." Jace began in exasperation.

"Pigheadedness goes hand in glove with being opinionated. Didn't you know?" She gave him an acid smile.

"I know you're a gutless wonder if your response to a little disagreement is to cut and run."

"A *little* disagreement! You yelled at me."

"Of course I yelled at you. You washed my lucky glove. What the hell did you expect me to do?"

"Show a little understanding?"

"But I don't understand." He ran his fingers through his hair in vexation. "I completely fail to understand how any rational person could accidentally wash my lucky glove."

"It may have been your lucky glove, but it sure wasn't mine," she said ruefully.

"No." A reluctant smile lifted the corners of his mouth.

Christina slowly tossed a few more clothes into her suitcase. Now that her anger was receding, a sense of loss was creeping in. She was about to leave Jace. She swallowed against the sour taste of grief that filled her. It didn't matter, she tried to tell herself. Who wanted a man who thought you were opinionated and aggravating?

"Is this how you always handle an argument? By running away?"

"I don't get into arguments often enough to have a modus operandi," she said, trying to think of a single time she'd gotten into a shouting match with a man. She couldn't. Not one of the men she'd known over the years had had the ability to make her as furious as Jace did. Which was all the more reason to leave now, she tried to tell herself. To leave before her confused emotions got any more tangled up.

"Disagreement is a fact of life in any viable relationship," Jace insisted. "And I give you fair warning that you're going to have to learn to handle it better than running home to mother."

"My mother is in the south of France at the moment. I, on the other hand, am going to Boston."

"No, you're not. You're going to stay right here at the farm until the season's over."

"Oh? And what do you suggest I do instead? Give in to my first impulse and smack you one?"

"Let me give you a word of advice. Never hit someone bigger than you. What I suggest we do is discuss the situation rationally now that we've both cooled off."

"Have we?" She eyed him narrowly. He did appear to be a lot calmer.

"We have, and now it's time for the next stage of our argument."

"Oh?" Christina felt an upsurge of excitement at the gleaming lights sparkling to life in his eyes.

"Uh-huh." He slowly stalked her. "We've reached the kiss-and-make-up stage."

Christina backed up until she felt the bed against her legs. "Ha! Your mother strikes again."

"Partly." He reached around her and swept her suitcase onto the floor. "But the embellishments are all my own." He gently tumbled her onto her bed.

The last remnants of Christina's anger melted away under the impact of his hard body. Blindly she reached for his head, eager to feel his lips against hers.

"Did I ever tell you, you have the best ideas?" she whispered against his parted lips.

"Darling, you haven't seen anything yet," he vowed as his mouth claimed hers.

Ten

We're never going to get off this plane," Albert moaned as he leaned into the aisle and stared forward toward the front of the packed 747.

"We were lucky to have gotten a seat on this flight at all," Christina pointed out. "All the other Sunday morning flights to L.A. would have arrived too late for us to see the game."

"We should have left yesterday." Albert bounced impatiently as the front of the plane slowly emptied.

"You were in school yesterday," Christina said, trying to stifle the sense of unease she felt as she remembered that it had been Jace's vehement objections to Albert missing school that had put them on this flight. She'd been perfectly willing to take Albert out of classes for one day. It had seemed a minor price to pay for the privilege of seeing Jace again after the interminable past weeks while he'd been finishing the season with the team.

She couldn't believe how much she'd missed him. Missed his wry humor and his sharp intelligence. She'd even missed their bickering over his use of sprays on the garden. But most of all she'd missed his physical presence. Her breathing shortened as a tide of heat surged beneath her skin at the memory of their lovemaking. It was as if her body had become so attuned to his that she was no longer complete as a separate entity. Because she loved him. The surprising bit of self-knowledge bubbled up from her subconscious, gathering momentum as it rose, until it finally burst into her mind with compelling force.

No, her instinctive reaction was to deny it. She couldn't be in love with Jace McCormick. She just liked him a lot. Sure, to the point of obsession, she thought grimly, remembering the vast amounts of time she'd wasted simply daydreaming about him.

Christina took a deep, steadying breath and tried to think, but she couldn't seem to get past the fact that she was in love with Jace and probably had been since shortly after they'd arrived at his farm. She'd always had a strong physical reaction to him. It had been there from the very first time Elizabeth had introduced him to her four years ago. She'd handled her unwilling attraction then by the simple expedient of avoiding him—something that had been easy to do when Elizabeth and Howard had been alive. But their deaths had forced her into close proximity with Jace for the first time, and her initial response had grown upon closer acquaintance, not diminished. Of all the impossible complications, she let her breath out on a long whistling sigh.

"Don't worry, Christina," Albert misunderstood the source of her unease. "It'll be our turn to deplane any minute now."

Christina gave the boy a shaky smile, wondering what they'd find when they finally did meet Jace. Would he be pleased to see them? Unlike the trip to Cincinnati, Jace hadn't instigated this one. In fact, he'd been distinctly cool to her suggestion that she and Albert come West for the final game of the season. Only her refusal to take no for an answer had elicited his grudging consent.

But why had it been grudging? She worried the question around in her mind. Why didn't he want them to see him pitch again? It certainly wasn't because he wanted them out of his life. He'd been emphatic in his insistence that she and Albert remain at the farm while he finished the season.

She grimaced. She could speculate for hours and never come up with the correct motive behind his decision. If, indeed, he had a conscious motive for trying to keep her and Albert safely tucked out of sight in Indiana.

"Come on, Christina." Albert yanked his suitcase out from under his seat. "It's our turn to get off. I sure hope Jace didn't get tired of waiting."

Christina retrieved her own case and followed Albert down the narrow aisle, sharing none of his excitement. Now that she was actually here, her overwhelming impulse was to catch the first flight back. The unexpected discovery of her love for Jace had unnerved her. She felt exposed, vulnerable and very uncertain—of herself, of Jace and of the whole situation.

Unfortunately, the situation deteriorated almost immediately. In her anxiety over her newfound love, she'd forgotten how newsworthy Jace was. While waiting for them in the airport lounge, he'd attracted the attention of a reporter, who was busily trying to find out why Jace was there, as well as a crowd of autograph seekers. As a result, Jace's reception of her and Albert was hurried. After a perfunctory greeting, he hustled them through the crowd of curious well-wishers and into his car, which was parked in the taxi zone.

"Thanks for the loan of the parking space, fellows," Jace called to the small knot of taxi drivers standing by the door.

"Anytime, Jace," one of them yelled back. "Just you win that game for us today. The whole season's riding on it."

Hungrily Christina studied his lean features as they pulled away from the curb. His face seemed visibly thinner than it had been just two weeks ago, and his lips were compressed as if in tension. Tension because she was here when he hadn't wanted her to be or tension because the traffic they were driving through would frighten anyone?

Trying to find a neutral subject, she asked, "What did that man mean, the whole season?"

"Christina, don't you read the sports page?" Albert asked in disgust. "If Jace wins today and the Reds beat San Diego, the Lancers win the Western division title."

"You mean to tell me you've been playing ball since last April and it all comes down to one game?" she asked incredulously.

"Only because I got injured." Jace grimaced in self-disgust. "I should have won three or four more games and then it wouldn't even be close."

"There are a lot of other players on the Lancers, too. If they'd done their jobs, you wouldn't have had to win a few more games," Christina said tartly, just beginning to fully appreciate the pressure he was under to win today.

"Yes, but I'm the name. I'm the one they expect to deliver."

"God helps those who help themselves. Anyway, it's only a game." She ignored the identical pair of incredulous eyes trained on her. Honestly, she thought, the way they carried on you'd think it was a matter of life and death. Whereas, if the truth were told, she'd just as soon Jace lost today. That way he could come home with them instead of still having to play the National League championships, to say nothing of the World Series. Always provided, of course, that he wanted them to stay with him a while longer. She and Albert did have to return to Boston sometime, she reminded herself. The weekly phone calls from the Walsingham school were becoming increasingly acrimonious.

"Jace'll win," Albert said confidently.

"And if he doesn't, the sun will still rise tomorrow," Christina pointed out.

"Will you care if I'm not a winner?" Jace shot her a curiously penetrating look.

"You're a winner, and that fact has nothing whatsoever to do with some stupid ball game. Now then—" she hurriedly changed the subject, afraid that she might have said too much "—where are we going? The stadium?" She glanced at her watch.

"No, you're still on Central Time. It's two hours earlier out here. I'll drop you off at my apartment."

"You aren't coming with us?" Albert's mournful voice echoed Christina's feelings exactly. How could she gauge his feelings for her if she couldn't get him alone? Unless he was purposefully doing this to avoid being alone with her. His next words relieved that particular worry.

"I have to be at the ballpark at least two hours before the game, Albert. I go over each batter on the other team's roster with the pitching coach and my catcher. We decide how I'm going to pitch to them."

"Oh?" Albert sounded surprised. "I didn't know you did all that beforehand. I thought you just pitched."

"Flinging that little white ball," he said with a wry look at Christina, "is the final stage in a helluva lot of preparation."

"Do you have a second car we can use to drive to the stadium?" Christina asked.

"No, and even if I did, I wouldn't want you out in L.A. traffic alone. I've arranged for a taxi to pick you up and take you to the ballpark. You can come home with me."

"But when you win there'll be a big party and we'll have to wait forever," Albert objected.

"If we win," Jace corrected. "And even if we do, I intend to slip out as soon as possible. I've never been a big fan of being doused with champagne."

"I think it'd be fun. Can I come into the locker room afterward?" Albert begged.

"No," Jace refused before Christina could. "I'm even less a fan of dousing kids with champagne."

"Aw, gee. I never get to have any fun," Albert grumbled.

"Here we are." Jace ignored him, pulling up in front of a towering high rise. "The guard at the desk will take you up to my apartment, Christina. I've already spoken to him."

"Can't you come up just for a minute?" Albert pleaded, and Christina held her breath, willing Jace to accept.

"Sorry, I'm already late and if I went upstairs with you…" He shot an intense look at Christina, setting off an answering spark deep within her. As if compelled by a force beyond her control, she leaned across the gearshift toward him, and his large hand closed around the back of her neck, gently pulling her into his embrace. His lips met hers, and his tongue surged inside her mouth as if seeking sustenance. The blind driving hunger fueling his kiss seemed to dissolve the hard knot of anxiety and uncertainty she'd been feeling since her precipitous discovery that she loved him. He might not return her love, but he wanted her. Their physical bond still burned with a mind-searing intensity.

"Not that again." Albert's disgusted voice penetrated Christina's fog of sensual pleasure a second before the sound of a camera clicking did. Startled, she lifted her head and blinked, trying to focus her passion-blurred eyes.

"Damn." Jace's whispered curse shook her a moment until she realized that it wasn't directed at her. He was looking past her at a pudgy little man standing beside the car and holding a large camera.

"I'm sorry, Christina." Jace ran his fingers through his hair in barely suppressed anger. "I should have realized that the press might be hanging around my apartment. Unfortunately, once I start to kiss you, my common sense flies out the window." His eyes lingered longingly on her lips.

"Come on. I'll run the gauntlet with you and Albert. Once you're inside the lobby, you'll be safe."

Jace climbed out of the car and, walking around the hood, opened the door for them.

"Who's the woman and the kid, Jace?" the reporter demanded. "An embarrassing reminder of the past?" he persisted when Jace ignored him.

"Hey, kid, is Jace your dad?"

Albert turned and glared at the obnoxious little man. "I am Howard Albert Hollowell the fourth and you're a—"

"Thoroughly despicable representative of an honorable profession." Jace's judicious comment rather surprisingly seemed to fluster the man.

"Aw, come on, Jace. I gotta have a story."

"Even if you have to make one up?" Christina said angrily, slipping through the lobby door Jace held open for them.

"Till later." Shielding her with his body, Jace dropped a quick kiss on her tingling lips.

"Break a leg," she called after him as he sprinted for his car.

"Break a—" Albert stared at her in horror.

"You say it for luck," she explained.

"Well, it's a cinch you don't say it for common sense," Albert said in disgust.

"Never mind." Christina turned to the security guard who was approaching them. "Let's go up to Jace's apartment and rest a while before we have to leave for the game."

"I'm not tired," Albert protested.

"Well, I am. I'm getting too old to enjoy flights that leave at the crack of dawn. You can amuse yourself while I take a nap." Because with any luck at all I won't be getting much sleep tonight, she thought dreamily, her pulse quickening at what she hoped would happen once they managed to dispose of this infernal ball game that everyone seemed so hyper about.

"There! There he is!" Albert shrieked with excitement as Jace slowly walked to the mound.

"Yup," Christina agreed, studying him with a critical eye. Her first impression had been right. He really was thinner. He needed to stop eating restaurant food and start living like a normal person. But he wasn't exactly a normal person, the reverberating screams from the standing-room-only crowd reminded her. To a lot of baseball fans he was some kind of demigod. She felt a shiver of apprehension chill her skin. She didn't understand this almost idolatrous attitude of the crowd toward him, and she most assuredly didn't like it. She liked the way they seemed to feel that they were entitled to all the details of his personal life even less.

"Way to go, Jace!" Albert screamed, and Christina looked up in time to see a batter walking back to the visitor's dugout.

Jace glanced over at them, a slight smile lifting his lips.

That was an improvement, Christina thought, smiling back. In Cincinnati he hadn't seemed to be aware of the fact that they were even in the same ballpark.

"Augh," Albert moaned as the next batter singled to left on the first pitch.

"He can't get everybody out," Christina consoled the little boy.

"Sure he can," Albert argued. "Jace's got more perfect games than any active player in either league."

"How nice," Christina murmured uncomprehendingly. "What's a—"

"She gasped in horror as the next batter lined a shot inches from Jace's head.

"Drat," Albert grumbled. "That's two on."

"Jace was almost decapitated, and all you're worried about is who's sitting on what base!"

"It missed him and we got to win or the season's over."

"Every cloud has its silver lining," Christina said, ignoring Albert's disgusted look. As far as she was concerned, the season couldn't end soon enough. Baseball was a dangerous sport.

"Don't worry, young man." The elderly gentleman sitting beside Albert reassured him. "McCormick'll settle down. He's pitching with only two days' rest, you know."

To Albert's loudly voiced relief, Jace did settle down, managing to retire the side with no further trouble. The game continued smoothly, although to Christina's disappointment, Jace never so much as glanced their way again. It almost seemed as if he were deliberately ignoring them. Telling herself that things were bad enough without her developing paranoia, she forced herself to follow the game.

Except for a solo home run a teammate of Jace's belted over the center field wall, nothing exciting happened until the middle of the seventh inning when it was announced that the Reds had beaten San Diego. The noise was deafening as the crowd reacted and then sat back to watch the game with an intensity that was almost tangible. They hung on Jace's every pitch as if the very force of their desire could protect his one-run lead.

By the ninth inning the tension was horrendous. Christina could feel it pressing in on her, and she was simply an anonymous member of the audience. What Jace must be feeling defied the imagination.

"Only two more to go, Jace," Albert screamed as the first batter went down on strikes.

The second man up hit a long fly to center that the outfielder caught, and Christina began to relax, although the same couldn't be said of the crowd. From what she could see, she was the only person actually sitting in the whole stadium.

Jace wound up and threw the ball over the outside of the plate. The batter hit a dribbler toward second. Jace ran to first to cover the bag, and Christina closed her eyes in a silent prayer that it was finally over. Jace had done what had been demanded of him. He'd won.

The hushed silence suddenly penetrated her happiness, and she opened her eyes to see Jace lying beside the first base bag with the batter sprawled across him.

"The bastard! That wasn't even a legal slide. He left the base path." The obscenity from the immaculately dressed old man added to her general sense of unreality.

"What happened? Why isn't Jace moving?" she demanded frantically as Lancers' players poured out of the dugout and raced toward him.

"The batter was trying to make Jace drop the ball," Albert explained. "So he slid into him."

"Oh, my God." Christina took a deep breath, trying to steady her racing heart.

The batter was gesturing wildly to the umpire while the crowd merely sat in stunned silence. Not so Albert. He leaned over the railing separating him from the field and screamed, "Lynch the batter!"

For once, Christina made no attempt to restrain his more bloodthirsty impulses. If that man really had hurt Jace, hanging was too good for him.

Her feeling of helplessness increased as one of the men around Jace moved and she caught a glimpse of the pain etched on Jace's face.

"Ten to one it's his knee," the elderly man echoed her concern. "He went straight for it."

The crowd drew a collective sigh as a stretcher was brought out of the dugout and Jace was carefully loaded onto it. As his teammates carried him off the field, the crowd burst into hysterical applause, but Christina barely heard it. She couldn't seem to get past the thought that Jace was hurt and she didn't even know where they were taking him. Somehow, she had to find out. She had to— "Miss Hollowell?" A middle-aged man in a suit demanded her attention.

"Yes?" She turned eagerly to him, hoping for information.

"I'm Dale Cartwright from the Lancers front office. Jace asked me to take you over to the hospital. That is, if you want to come?"

"Try and stop me." She gave him a relieved smile as some of her fears began to melt. Jace had thought of her even in his pain.

"And you must be Albert." Dale won the boy's heart by formally shaking his hand. "Jace said you have the makings of a fine soccer player."

"Did he?" Albert seemed to swell with pride and then, suddenly remembering, asked, "What's wrong with him?"

"Yeah, what's wrong with him?" a woman farther down the row, who'd been openly eavesdropping, demanded.

"It's his knee again." Dale ignored the woman and addressed Christina. "But exactly how bad it is..." He grimaced. "That kid deliberately went for it."

"Why would he do that?" Albert asked angrily. "Even if they won the ball game, it wouldn't help them any in the standings."

"Who knows?" He shrugged. "The kid's a rookie. Maybe he was trying to make an impression."

"He made an impression on me, all right!" Christina snapped.

"We shoulda lynched him," Albert muttered.

Dale chuckled. "Tempting as the idea is, the Commissioner's Office frowns on things like that. Now, if you'll both come with me..."

With the help of three ushers, Dale cleared a path for them through the crowd and led them out a back entrance to the stadium marked Fire Exit Only. "You, young man, are going to go home with Dave. You remember Dave, don't you?" Dale asked.

"Yeah, he's nice, but I want to go to the hospital with Christina and see Jace," Albert protested.

"It'll be hours before she'll be able to see him, and Jace didn't want you to have to hang around all that time with nothing to do," Dale soothed him. "I promise that just as soon as we hear anything definite, I'll call you. In the meantime you could try to keep Dave's mind off things. He's worried, too. Good roommates are hard to find, you know."

"I guess." Albert agreed although it was obvious he was far from satisfied. A feeling Christina shared. If Dale was expecting it to be hours before they knew anything, then it was obvious that it was a whole lot more than just a sprain or a pulled ligament.

"Bill'll drive you to the hospital, Miss Hollowell." Dale gently shepherded her toward the car parked beside the exit. "And don't worry about Albert. We'll take good care of him."

"And you take good care of Jace, Christina." Albert gave her a suffocating hug.

"I will. I promise." She hugged him back and then climbed into the car.

She arrived at the hospital twenty minutes later and walked into a scene straight out of a disaster movie. The lobby was packed with people, many of whom were carrying cameras. Christina was subjected to a quick assessment and then dismissed as nonnewsworthy.

She breathed a sigh of relief that the picture taken of her and Jace kissing that morning had not as yet hit the newsstands. In her present state of mind she'd never have been able to fend off their persistent questions without making enemies. Enemies Jace wouldn't thank her for.

Christina glanced around the packed room, trying to get her bearings. The driver had told her to go to the reception desk and give them her name, and that Dale had left word that she was to be taken straight up to orthopedics. Locating the desk, she started to thread her way through the mass of bodies.

Finally reaching it, she accosted the woman on duty. "Excuse me, but—"

"Mr. McCormick is in surgery and I have no information on his condition at this time," the woman rattled off without even bothering to look up.

"Surgery?" Christina's startled voice caught the woman's attention and she glanced up, frowning at Christina's shocked features.

"What paper are you with?" she asked.

"None, my name is Christina Hollowell and—"

"Well, why didn't you say so before." The woman depressed a button on her desk. "I thought you belonged to that group of vultures." She glared at the newsmen crowding in around Christina.

"Come on, lady. Give us a break. We're only trying to do our job." One of the reporters took exception to her description.

She ignored him, beckoning to an orderly who was making his way through the crowd to them.

"John, run this lady up to orthopedics, would you?" she asked him.

"Hey, why does she get to go up and we don't?" a reporter behind Christina demanded.

"Because she's a member of the human race," the harassed woman snapped. "The rest of you I'm not so sure about."

"I'll give you a hundred bucks if you'll call my editor with the latest information on McCormick's condition." A man tried to shove a bill at Christina. "My newspaper is—"

Christina brushed past him, intent only on getting up to Jace as soon as possible.

"Kind of scary, isn't it?" The orderly shuddered once they'd reached the relative safety of the elevator.

"It certainly is," Christina agreed wholeheartedly.

"Here we are." John held the elevator door open for her when they reached the fourth floor. "Orthopedics is straight ahead. Just tell them who you are."

"Thank you for your help." Christina gave him a sincere if somewhat abstracted smile and hurried down the hall to orthopedics where she was met by a middle-aged nurse who merely repeated the information about Jace being in surgery.

"Yes, but what are they operating for?" Christina persisted.

The nurse studied Christina's tense features for a second and said, "You must be someone pretty special to Jace if the team's front office is looking out for you?"

"I don't know how special I am to him, but he's the whole world to me," Christina said, feeling an enormous relief in actually saying the words aloud.

"Isn't that just like a man?" the woman snorted. "They never want to commit themselves. Tell you what. You can wait in his room instead of in the ward waiting room with everyone else. When he gets back from the recovery room, he'll still be groggy. You wangle a declaration out of him, and I'll be your witness if he tries to renege."

Christina grinned at her. "Thanks, but I think they got rid of breach-of-promise suits."

"Pity." The woman shook her head. "He'd do better with you, because it's a cinch his pitching days are over."

"What?" Christina felt a clutch of fear squeeze her heart.

"Well, this is just between you and me, but Angie, one of the surgical nurses, saw his X rays and she says his kneecap is shattered."

"Shattered?" Christina turned chalk white and there was an ominous buzzing in her ears.

"Hey, take it easy. Our Dr. Wellington can fix it. It's just like putting a jigsaw puzzle back together again, you know," she said encouragingly.

"No, I don't know." Christina took a deep breath.

"Now, don't you worry. You go sit in Mr. McCormick's room and wait. It's 426. Right down there." She pointed down the hall. "Would you like me to bring you a cup of coffee?"

"No, thank you." Christina forced her shaky legs to carry her to his room.

The next three hours passed with agonizing slowness as Christina paced up and down the small private room, much too nervous to sit still. She couldn't quite shake the feeling that something had gone terribly wrong. Surely it didn't take that long to fix one small kneecap. Especially if the surgeon really was as good as that nurse seemed to think. Maybe Jace had had a reaction to the anesthetc? Maybe he'd died on the operating table and they'd forgotten she was in here waiting for him to come back? All the horror stories she'd ever heard about surgical catastrophes came storming out of her memory to plague her. She was about to find a nurse and beg for more information when she heard the rattle of a gurney's wheels a second before the door was pushed open.

"Here's your wandering lad." The friendly nurse beamed at her. "He came through the operation with flying colors. Now you move out of the way while we get him into his bed so he can rest."

"Rest! In this chamber of horrors!" Jace's voice was the only thing about him that seemed normal. His pain-filled eyes burned like brown coals in his pale face, an IV tube had been inserted in his left hand, and the plaster around his injured knee made it appear three times normal size.

"Now, now." The nurse twitched his sheet into place and with a conspiratorial wink at Christina left, taking the two orderlies with her.

Christina approached the bed, drawn by the appeal in Jace's overly bright eyes. Slowly she reached out and lightly stroked his white cheek. To her surprise, she burst into tears.

"Christina!" Jace sounded horrified. Awkwardly reaching out, he grasped her hand and squeezed it comfortingly. "Don't cry, love," he pleaded. "It isn't that bad. And I did get the guy out."

"Who the hell cares whether he's out or not?" She cried all the harder. "Look what he did to your knee."

"I'm not so sure he didn't do me a backhanded favor," Jace said cryptically.

"Oh? You're into pain?" She sniffed disconsolately. "Maybe Albert was right. Maybe we should just have lynched him."

"Buck up. It's not the end of the world," Jace insisted. "My baseball career may be over, but once my knee's healed, the doctor says it'll be fine for most things. I mean, it's not like I lost anything irreplaceable, like you."

Christina stared into his face, trying to decipher his exact meaning. She couldn't. The lingering effects of the anesthetic, as well as the pain that he was obviously feeling, were obliterating all signs of any other emotion.

"Am I irreplaceable?" she forced the question out.

"Without you I don't have any future," he said flatly. "If you won't marry me, I don't know how I'm going to get through the rest of my life."

"Oh, Jace. Do you mean it? You aren't just saying it because of Albert?" A tiny shred of doubt remained.

Jace threaded his chilled fingers through her much warmer ones. "The only reason I'm asking you to marry me is because I love you to distraction. I know Albert is safe with you. You'll do a fine job of raising him just as I hope you'll do a fine job of raising any children we might be lucky enough to have."

"Oh, Jace. I love you so much, and I was so afraid you wouldn't want any kind of long-term commitment," she blurted out her fears.

"And all the time I've been madly plotting how to tie you to me with every device I could think of. If you want to know how much you fill my thoughts, just remember the first inning."

"The first inning?" Christina frowned in confusion.

"I looked over at you, and suddenly all I could think about was kissing you and the feel of your warm body beneath mine and the soft little sounds you make when—"

"Jace!" She glanced nervously toward the door.

He chuckled. "I don't care if the whole world knows how I feel about you. But the point I'm trying to make is that you distracted me from my pitching. In eighteen years nothing has ever disturbed my concentration, and yet all it took was a glimpse of you out of the corner of my eye. I had to use every ounce of willpower I owned to keep from looking at you again."

"Jace, if you feel that way about me, why did you try to keep us from coming out here for the game?"

"Because you were already leery about me as a baseball player. Hell, I saw what happened in Cincinnati. I was so used to the fans that I never stopped to consider how you'd react. But you just sort of...withdrew from me. Why do you think I went back to the farm with you? I was desperate to recoup lost ground. I was afraid if I traveled on with the team as I was supposed to, you'd have time to erect defenses against me. So I told the team's general manager that if he wanted my enthusiastic cooperation for the rest of the pennant drive, he'd better let me spend the days before my next start with you."

"Didn't he mind?"

Jace grimaced. "Let's just say it wasn't his favorite idea, but you were more important to me than baseball."

"I love you, Jace McCormick." Her incandescent smile illuminated her face. "All I want to do is make love to you.

And I can't even kiss you properly without fear of hurting you." She glared in frustration at his heavily bandaged knee.

"I'm beginning to think Albert had the right idea after all," Jace said ruefully. "We should have lynched that batter."

*   *   *   *   *

Silhouette Desire

COMING NEXT MONTH

DARING MOVES
Linda Lael Miller

Painful pasts brought Amanda and Jordan together. But when her ex-lover and Jordan's two small daughters turned up, Amanda's and Jordan's passion was challenged in a way that neither had anticipated …

CONTACT
Lass Small

Once badly burnt, Ann Forbes now steered clear of men, especially powerhouse types like Clint Burrows. But Clint didn't feel like a hotshot. He felt like a man in love. How could he assail Ann's defenses?

RUBY FIRE
Celeste Hamilton

Aunt Eugenia strikes again! This time she sets out to rekindle love's flame between fiery Cassandra Martin and stoic Daniel O'Grady, in Book Two of Aunt Eugenia's Treasures.

Silhouette Desire

COMING NEXT MONTH

LOCK, STOCK AND BARREL
Cathryn Clare

It was the perfect end to a rotten day! Maggie Lewis's purse had been snatched and she couldn't get into her car. Connor Blake came to the rescue, but he was reluctant to enter Maggie's world.

HEARTBREAK HOTEL
Jackie Merritt

An attempt to prevent her grandfather from making an awful mistake brought KC into conflict with the law in the form of alarmingly attractive Sheriff Pierce Wheeler. However, Pierce was definitely more interested in the granddaughter than the grandfather!

A LOVING SPIRIT
Annette Broadrick

Sabrina Sheldon's guardian angel was working overtime. Sabrina needed a man in her life, but she seemed totally unaware of the fact. Even after meeting Michael Donovan, Sabrina was resisting her destiny.

A Free Silhouette novel for you!

At Silhouette we always do our best to ensure that our books are just what you want to read. To do this we need your help! Please spare a few minutes to answer the questions below and overleaf and, as a special thank you, we will send you a FREE Silhouette romance when you return your completed questionnaire.

Don't forget to fill in your name and address so we know where to send your FREE BOOK.

Please tick the appropriate boxes to indicate your answers. ✔

1 **How long have you been reading Silhouette novels?**

	Less than 1 year	1-2 years	3-5 years	More than 5 years	I don't read this series
Special Edition	❏	❏	❏	❏	❏
Desire	❏	❏	❏	❏	❏
Sensation	❏	❏	❏	❏	❏

2 **How often do you read each series?**

	Every month	Every 2-3 months	Every 6 months	Once a yr or less	I don't read this series
Special Edition	❏	❏	❏	❏	❏
Desire	❏	❏	❏	❏	❏
Sensation	❏	❏	❏	❏	❏

3 **Which of the series, if any, is your favourite?**

Special Edition ❏ Desire ❏
Sensation ❏ Like them all equally ❏

4 **Why is this your favourite?**_____

_____

_____

5 **Do you read historical romances** Yes ❏ No ❏

Please complete overleaf

6. How often, if at all, do you read any of the following Mills & Boon novels?

	Every month	2-3 months	Every 6 months	Once a yr or less	I don't read this series
M&B Romance	❑	❑	❑	❑	❑
M&B Temptation	❑	❑	❑	❑	❑
M&B Medical Romance	❑	❑	❑	❑	❑
M&B Best Seller	❑	❑	❑	❑	❑
M&B Collection	❑	❑	❑	❑	❑

7. Where do you get your Silhouette books from?

	Special Edition	Desire	Sensation
Reader Service	❑	❑	❑
Buy new from the shops	❑	❑	❑
Buy secondhand	❑	❑	❑
Borrow from library	❑	❑	❑
Borrow from a friend / relation / colleague	❑	❑	❑

8. So that we know a bit about you please tick the boxes that apply to you:

Age group Under 25 ❑ 25-34 ❑ 35-44 ❑ 45-54 ❑ 55-64 ❑ 65+ ❑

Employment	Marital status	Children
Student ❑	Single ❑	No children ❑
Work part-time ❑	Divorced ❑	Children of pre-school age ❑
Work full-time ❑	Married ❑	Children of school age ❑
Full-time housewife ❑	Co-habitating ❑	Children have left home ❑
Unemployed ❑	Widowed ❑	
Retired ❑		

9. Do you think you might be interested in taking part in any future research that we carry out on Silhouette books?

Yes, I might be interested in any research by post ❑

Yes, I might be interested in any research discussions ❑

No thank-you, I am not interested in any further research ❑

Thank you for your help. We hope that you enjoy your FREE book.

Post this page TODAY TO: Silhouette Survey FREEPOST, P.O. Box 236, Croydon CR9 9EL.

Mrs/Ms/Miss/Mr_____ **SILQ**

Address_____

_____

_____

Postcode _____